The Hotel Bellman

By Sherman Cain

Sherman Cain
cainsherman23@gmail.com
San Leandro, CA

Contributors:
Front Cover Art: Howard Jao
Back Cover Photography: Sherman Cain
Editing & Formatting: Lorraine Castle

ISBN-13: 978-0-692-28637-1
ISBN-10: 0692286373

14 15 16 17 18 SC 10 9 8 7 6 5 4 3 2 1

Acknowledgements

I would like to recognize the most important person in my life, God, who I owe all my blessings to.

Regina Dilelio who has an attentive eye for what was good and bad in writing this story and who inspired me to continue writing through the most perplexing times. Thank you, love, for being in my life.

My ever-loving parents, Minnie and Sherman.

My children Sydney, Shermaine and Makeda Cain who give me the joy of being a father.

To Ruby Bradley-Cain and Osmond Cain, without your belief and support, I could not have finished this journey.

Love you all!

Prologue

Shamar is a midlife gentleman who is determined to overcome all the obstacles he endured while growing up. You see, Shamar is a witty and personable character whose self-esteem puts him above all other guests at the office party. Co-workers and hotel guests would gather around his presence to be amazed by the satirical and humorous stories he would tell about his adventures as a child, in marriage, and in life. Whatever the subject was, he would captivate the audience.

Now when Shamar went to apply for a job as "Guest Service Aide" at the largest room hotel in the city, he didn't realize the title meant taking on a job as a Bellman; however, he was excited. He thought his charm and intellect would carry him to the great fortunes in tips and acquaintances. Explore the journey with the Bellman and be amazed by the immoral and illegal things he does for the sake of making a tip.

Contents

Introduction

The weather was good for a fall day in the Midwest. The temperature was around 72 degrees Fahrenheit and strolling along the Mississippi River banks was serene. This was a day of solitude I had not enjoyed for as long as I could remember. It made all thoughts of the misfortunes I was experiencing go away. Looking at riverboat casinos made me wish I had enough money in my pocket to go aboard and try my luck at the game of chances. However, this was one of the many dreams I had while sitting on the bank gazing at the skyline of the great Metropolitan City.

You see, I had been unemployed for almost a year. Although I was receiving weekly unemployment benefits from a previous job, I knew that after that was exhausted; I'd be a casualty of the world economic recession. The national unemployment rate was at ten percent, and the chances of a 50-year-old man finding a job were slim. With this realization in mind, I hit the pavement, searching for employment. I asked myself the question, "What do I apply for?" The days of signs in the window saying "Help Wanted" were over.

While walking the downtown business district of the city, I noticed that at every other corner there was a hotel and "Bingo!" – a thought came to my mind. This would be a great industry to work in because I had experience in customer service and the food service. I decided to try my luck and apply for a job at the next hotel I saw. Before proceeding, I got down on my knees and prayed to God for another chance in life.

As I continued walking, I came upon this magnificent five-star hotel called the "The Grandeur." Little did I know this was the largest hotel in the city, though I noticed the line of airport limos and cars swelling at its entrance. The Doormen and Bellmen were at a frenzy trying to accommodate the constant flow of guests trying to check in. As I continued to make my way inside the hotel I became elated with the decision I made to apply for a job here. The lobby looked like the entrance to a Grand Palace. At this time, I knew this was where I needed to work.

At the front desk, I was asked by a well-dressed gentleman if he could help me. Of course, my response was that I was here to see if they had any job openings. He suggested that I go search the web and see what was available. While talking to this gentleman, an old friend of mine came out of the hotel office and greeted me. She was a girl who I grew up with in my old neighborhood and she offered to escort me down to the computer room.

Now at this time, while conversing with her, she suggested that I apply for a job they had opened as a Guest Service Aide (otherwise known as a Bellman). She went on to tell me that it was a great job and I could earn quite a bit of money in tips. I knew that maybe she could give me a good recommendation since she was one of the employees there. When we got to the computer, she explained to me how to operate it and apply for the job I desired. As I continued to scroll through the job listings, she told me that after I applied she would talk with the Front Office Manager and put in a good word for me.

After submitting my application, I left the hotel excited. I stopped again to kneel on my knees and pray to the Lord that he bless me with this job. Realizing that I had only one unemployment benefit check left to receive, I foresaw the days of despair upon me. It was a depressing feeling, seeing yourself without an income. Believe me – I've been there. The most disheartening thing about it is that I lived at home with my 85-year-old mother who I helped take care of. My mother was struck by a car 30 years before while crossing the street and sustained serious injuries that left her disabled.

Walking home from the hotel, I knew it was time for me to prepare lunch for my mother, and that she was patiently watching and looking out of the window waiting for my arrival. Although I had other siblings, they lived out of town and all her needs were dependent on me. With her mere social security check, she relied on me to fill the gap when it was bill time. Therefore, I always had to keep cash on hand in case of unforeseen expenses. This was why I was so desperately looking for a job: so I could continue to take care of my mother.

The next day, my cell phone rang. I didn't recognize the number, nor did it identify who was calling, so I reluctantly answered. To my surprise, it was the assistant manager of the front office of The Grandeur, and he asked when I would be available for an interview. He made it clear that he desperately needed a good Bellman. My response was that I was able to come in today since I didn't have anything else more important than to come in for a possible job. We set a time of 2:00 pm for that same day. After we hung up I shouted, "Thank You, God!" because I knew, he was going to bless me with this job.

I jumped out of bed and went to tell my mother the good news about the interview. She was so happy for me and immediately pulled me down on my knees to pray; she said, "Father, we give you praises for the life you have given us. Thank you for my son Shamar, who's been at my side in time of need. We need not ask you what our needs are – you already know. Bless Shamar with this job totally so he can continue to live a constructive and productive life."

This was a beautiful day for me. I felt so joyous. You see, I hadn't been happy with my life over the past year. My wife had left me for a younger man, I was fired from my job as a city health inspector, and I really hadn't been able to provide financially for my disabled mother. My mother stayed in a small two-bedroom apartment that wasn't handicap equipped. After her accident, she was unable to walk without the aid of a walker, so I had to give up my apartment to move in with her. She needed someone around to help her prepare her meals and keep her apartment clean. That was my job as her son.

Well, things were looking better for us now because I felt I would be hired for this job as a Bellman. My friend from the hood said she was going to give me a good recommendation and inside support is always a plus. So I made sure to dress to impress at my interview. I looked in my closet and got my favorite suit out. It was a navy blue pinstripe two-button suit with pleated slacks. I hooked this up with a powder blue shirt and a paisley navy blue tie. Lookout – I was confident I would prevail!

As I left home for my interview, it was another beautiful day. The temperature was 70 degrees Fahrenheit and the neighborhood was active with people sitting out on their porches, washing their cars, playing music, etc. However, while on my way to the interview of my life, negative thoughts began to enter my mind. What if, when I arrived, they took into account that I'm in my 50's? Usually, Bellmen are younger guys in their

20's and 30's. Only the Doorman is often older. What if they did a criminal background check on me? I'd had some problems with the law some 35 years ago, and if they did a credit history check on me, I was a goner.

But I shook all these negative thoughts off my mind and began to think positive things. I began thinking how much of an asset I would be for this hotel. For instance, I was academically inclined and had a college degree. I was socially orientated, humorous, and above all, without being conceited, I was a handsome guy. I was hygienic and a sharp dresser. So I thought, why wouldn't they hire someone with my standards? Remembering all of these positive attributes, I started feeling good about myself again. I knew when they saw me they would be impressed. This was the attitude I must go in the door with.

Upon my arrival at The Grandeur, I had a sense of confidence. However, I couldn't help thinking of the days I spent walking downtown searching for work. The days and nights I spent on my laptop applying for jobs I was never called for – it was a frustrating experience. I entered the hotel lobby and was greeted by a Bellman named Vito. He thought I was a guest checking in and offered his service to me. I informed him that I wasn't there as a guest, but for a 2:00 PM interview with Mr. Gentry.

Vito summoned the manager and I was elated to see that he was an older gentleman like me. He appeared to be around

60 years of age and had a great swagger with his walk. This brief encounter with him gave my ego reassurance that my age would not be a discriminating factor in this process. Now, as Vito walked in the back office of the hotel, my old friend came out to greet me. She informed me she was too busy to chitchat, but assured me that she gave me a good reference and to relax, I'll get the job.

The Interview

Sitting in the lobby of this large and magnificent hotel, I was amazed by the constant flow of guests, who were moving about trying to check in and out of their temporary residence. The guest check-in agents moved at a zealous pace to keep up with the long line of guests. As I was watching this congestive atmosphere, a gentleman came over and introduced himself as Mr. Ron Gentry (Assistant Front Desk Manager). When I stood to acknowledge him, he gave me a flattering compliment on my attire and the aroma of cologne I was wearing.

This first impression gave me the confidence I needed to get relaxed for this interview. Mr. Gentry led me back to his office and we proceeded to start our dialogue. The first question he asked was for me to tell him something about myself and what made me qualified for this job as a Bellman. My response was that it was obvious that he had to be selective in choosing the right candidate for this job but that I could make a positive contribution to this hotel.

I told him I had an extensive background in different areas and had numerous skills and qualities that would be useful to the hotel industry. My experience as a Health Inspector had helped perfect my interpersonal and communication skills, which were also necessary in owning and running my own business. I had gained excellent customer service and management experience and learned the importance of being very detail-oriented. I continued to tell him that being an entrepreneur also enhanced my people skills and helped me realize the importance of being a team player, which this job requires.

At this time, I noticed that Mr. Gentry's attention was fixed on my ability to intelligently use grammar and make eye contact with him. After I saw he was transfixed with my conversation, I thought I would conclude by letting him know that the day-to-day duties of running my own business had given me qualities that will be useful to the position he had available. When we finished, Mr. Gentry told me he would contact me later because he had other interviews to conduct. With a conflicted look on his face, he told me to sit back down and asked did I have time to meet his boss and, of course, I said yes.

Approximately five minutes later, Mr. Gentry reappeared and led me to another office where a neatly dressed gentleman was typing at a computer. Without looking up at me, he offered me a seat and introduced himself as Terry Daniels (Front Office Manager). Little did I know he was the last person to determine if I was hired or not. I was later informed that Mr. Gentry told his boss that I was a prime candidate for the job as a Bellman.

While sitting with Mr. Daniels, he told me that he had heard good things about me through one of his employees (my friend from the hood, Wendy). He also mentioned that Mr. Gentry was greatly impressed with our interview. Now, he just wanted to know where I saw myself in the next five years. I told him that after I learned all the skills of a Bellman, I would love to train as a Front Desk Agent. I explained to him that being social and helpful to people was one of my greatest strengths.

After talking non-stop about my desire to be a productive and dependable employee, he was impressed and immediately offered me the job. A glow came over me that the sun could not out-do. This was the period in my life that I felt anew. You see my life had been uncertain until this point. Remember, I was a 56-year-old man who didn't have any security for my retirement age. I was born during the baby boom era and shortly most of us will be out of the mainstream of life. Without life and health insurance, I would be a victim of government supplement health care, which is a sure way your health will deteriorate.

The excitement of knowing that I would finally be able to contribute to the company's 401 Profit Sharing Plan, and receive a full insurance package, had been a dream for me. Now that I was assured this wasn't a dream, I thanked THE LORD. Transfixed with the joyous thoughts for my future, I was finally able to respond to Mr. Daniels and give him my gratitude for the opportunity to work for The Grandeur.

Mr. Daniels explained the hiring process to me: first there would be a background check of past employers and criminal record check. After that was completed, I would have to pass a drug screening test, all of which I didn't have a problem with. After all these preliminaries were completed and satisfied, he told me, I would start a three day orientation of the hotel policies and procedures, rules and regulations. He concluded by saying I should be ready to start work in three weeks.

When our interview ended, I couldn't leave the hotel right then; I had to find my friend Wendy, who was instrumental in their decision to hire me. As I came out of the manager's office, I ran into her and she asked me how did my interview go? The only thing to do was to hug her and give her a big wet kiss. She said, "I see you got the job." I responded, "Yes I did, thanks to you."

Walking home from the hotel that day was the most joyous walk I had in my life. But before I left the grounds, I stopped in a familiar spot. It was the same place I stopped when I first entered the hotel to apply for the job I now had. I got down on my knees and said, "Thank you, God, for the day you have given me. Thank you for hearing my cry for you to come into my life. Bless my mother, father, children, and family members who need your rapture. Give me the strength to stay focused on my future endeavors you have blessed me with. Amen."

As I continued to walk home, which was only six blocks away, I couldn't believe that I might now be in the position to get my mother a bigger apartment on the ground floor so she wouldn't have to climb two flights of stairs anymore. My greatest thought was that now I would be able to purchase a vehicle so I could transport my mother to her doctor appointments and to the grocer, because she loved to go to the stores and shop. I would be overwhelmed to see her expression when I got home and told her that I finally got a job. Like I said, this was the greatest walk of my life.

The one objective I had in mind was how I was going to convince guests to be generous enough to give me a tip for my services. Although I hadn't started my job yet, I wanted to prepare myself for the various personalities I would encounter. Every person is different and for a man whose livelihood is going to depend on the generosity of others, you have to be able to read their body language. Perceiving a person's mood is very difficult. Throughout my life, I'd had to be a sociable and adventurous individual to attempt this evaluation.

We've all met someone who gave us a negative attitude. How about that person who appears to have a shield in front of them and you can't get in? Or how about passing a person with a frown on their face and being afraid to speak to them? My favorite is the person you greet and their response is irate and loud. All these encounters we've experienced throughout our lives, but rejection is the hardest thing for people to accept. However, I handle it very well. When it confronts you, patience is the virtue. Keep a smile on your face and thank them for their time anyway.

Most people are remorseful after they have insulted a person's feelings. After it appears to them that their offense upset you, they usually come back to apologize and offer their remorse. This is the attitude I plan to take on my job because I realize I'll be dealing with the public and all people have issues. You never know what mood you catch a person in, so you have to demonstrate your empathy to their cause. Although it may appear hard to withstand, I had to remember that my earnings would depend on my politeness and service to the guests.

It had been two weeks since my interview and I was getting a little impatient. All of a sudden, my cell phone rang, and it was Mr. Gentry from the hotel. My heart began to race with nervousness. I didn't know if I was excited or scared for bad news that I didn't pass the background check. When I answered, he informed me that I needed to come into the hotel and pick up a form at Human Resources so I could go take a drug screen testing. He informed me that after I passed that, I could begin orientation.

After Mr. Gentry hung up, I was relieved. It was not that I didn't think I was qualified, but my job was contingent upon my past employers' comments about my character. I had been fired from my last job for insubordination and that thought lingered in my mind. I also thought about that criminal conviction. But I didn't let these things discourage me because I knew that God had brought me this far and He wasn't going to forsake me now.

At this point, I was really convinced that this was my life. I couldn't wait to start my new job as a Bellman. I immediately proceeded to the hotel to pick up my forms for the drug screening, my last hurdle. Behind the hotel, I found an open door and slipped in. I didn't know this was the employee's entrance and I was immediately stopped by a Guest Response Officer. After explaining to him that I was a new employee going to HR to pick up some forms, he let me continue on my way. I was surprised to encounter so many people I personally knew who worked there at the hotel.

Everything in my life was so reassuring at this point. Two days after completing my final hurdle in landing this job, I received a call from HR telling me that my drug-screening test was positive and I would start orientation the next day. After this, I could start work immediately. It was Friday evening when I finished orientation and Monday was my day to finally report to work as a Bellman.

I went to sleep that night imagining how I would fill my pocket with tips. I gathered this from evaluating how busy this hotel appears to be and the guests they serviced were well off financially. If I just used charm and showed concern for their needs, I figured, I would win them over. The main thing that made this hotel famous was that it was adjacent to one of the largest convention centers in the western hemisphere. That meant that conventions for religious groups, college sororities, fraternities, Fortune 500 companies, and other organizations were always happening nearby. My endeavor was to make all the money possible by any means necessary. Nothing was going to stand in my way. I needed it…

Training Day

My first day as a Bellman fell on a Monday. As I approached the Front Desk of the hotel, I was mesmerized by the beauty of the clerk who greeted me. "Sir, welcome to The Grandeur Hotel. May I help you?" she said. I was transfixed by her doll's round face and black button eyes. Her shape was desirable for any woman walking down a model's runway. She appeared to be around 40 years old with a youth that was not diminished by her life. I finally responded that I was Shamar Moore and I was there to see Mr. Gentry. "I'm here to start work as the new Bellman," I said. She smiled gleaming and said, "Welcome, sir. He's expecting you. And may I ask what fragrance are you wearing?" I replied that it was "Usher®."

As I responded, Mr. Gentry came from out of his office and greeted me. He introduced me to the lady who I thought was a Front Desk Clerk, but she was a Bellman herself. "Shamar, I see you have already met Precious Johnson. She's one of our premier Bellpersons and she's going to be training you for the next three days." I was delighted, of course; her name was a perfect fit for her. I would not have a problem following her.

Mr. Gentry proceeded to escort me around the hotel, introducing me to all my new co-workers, which seemed to be unlimited. I was caught up in a celebrity atmosphere where everyone was excited to greet me.

The grandeur of the lobby was breathtaking. At the entrance stood two statues of bronze stallions uplifted with a sense of charging at you. The descending stairway to the lower level of the hotel was massive, with the center chandelier cascading down, giving you a feeling of royalty.

After our tour and introductions, I was finally released to Precious. "OK, Shamar, I'm going to leave you in the hands of Precious, our star Bellman and most experienced. Please be attentive to all of our procedures and service we provide our guests. Now I'll rest assured that Precious will do a magnificent job in training you and if there's any questions you have about anything; please don't hesitate to ask me," said Mr. Gentry. At this point, I was totally relaxed and very comfortable with the atmosphere of the hotel. The other Bellmen on duty that day welcomed me with the feeling of family. But my great enjoyment was that I would be working with Precious, who was very attractive and desirable.

When Mr. Gentry departed, Precious said, "Well, Shamar, tell me some things about you. What made you decide you wanted to be a Bellman at this point in your life? I see you're not a spring chicken. Let me first say that I hope you don't have any joint problems because this job requires you to stoop, bend, and lift, so if you have any aches and pains you better leave out the door immediately and save me some time. Your biggest problem today is going to be trying to keep up with me because guests are flowing in and you and nobody else is going to slow my paper down."

I was speechless. This was the woman who I thought was transparent of any insecurity in her life. Her attitude was the opposite of what I imagined it would be. However, I did not let this encounter discourage me from staying focused on my objective, and that was to be the best Bellman here and to make all the tips possible. Little did she know that I had taken this job with the intention of not letting anyone slow down *my* paper.

Precious went on to give me the protocol of how the Bellmen operated. She explained that when a guest first checks into the hotel we alternated who serviced that person. Without her going any further, I had to interject my feelings on her approach to our first encounter.

"Listen, Precious, slow down. It appears to me that you'd rather work alone and not have me as your trainee. Remember, Mr. Gentry assigned you to me, I didn't choose you. I don't even know you. Now, if you don't want to work with me, I'll tell Mr. Gentry to get another Bellman who's not as irritable as you are."

Before another word was uttered, Precious saw a guest walk into the hotel followed by the Doorman, who was pulling a loaded cart of luggage. Precious said to me, "Shamar, this is your first lesson on how we operate. Pay close attention and follow every move I make." After the Doorman placed the luggage cart in a designated area of the lobby, she showed me where we posted up until the guests had checked in and gotten their room key. After the new guest was finished at the Front Desk, Precious politely approached her and introduced herself as the Bellperson who would be assisting her.

"Good morning, Miss. Welcome to The Grandeur Hotel. My name is Precious and I'll be delighted to take your luggage to your room. What room number are we going to?" After the guest told Precious the room number, she grabbed the heavy luggage cart and began pulling it toward the elevator. I immediately started to follow Precious and the guest. As we entered the elevator, Precious introduced me. "Miss, this is Shamar Moore. He's our new Bellman and I'm training him today, so please don't be offended by his presence."

The guest looked over at me with a lovely smile, but didn't respond to the introduction. Upon arriving at her room, I stood at the door and watched Precious unload her luggage and stack her suitcases neatly near her closet. While she was doing this, I couldn't help but notice how the guest was focused on me as though I was servicing her. After Precious finished she said,

19

"Miss, is there anything else I can help you with?" The guest replied, "No, thank you!" while giving Precious a $20.00 tip.

While leaving my first guest room with Precious, she explained to me that during my training I wasn't allowed to earn any tips while in the company of another Bellman. This was discouraging for me on my first day on the job; however, I just concluded that those were the rules. It only gave me determination to be the best that I could be at this job. My only critique of Precious was how she first approached the guest.

The only thought I had in mind was how I would present myself to the guests to win them over. What I did know was that your first impression is your last impression: you must leave people with the memory of how delightful your personality is when you first greeted them. Precious did not demonstrate this at all. She did not extend her hand or smile when she first greeted the guest. Nor was her voice soft and gentle – it was hard and unconcerned of the guests' needs. I knew I had to pay close attention to the guests' reactions to the Bellman.

Precious and I continued working as a team that day. Every time she checked a guest in or out of the hotel, I followed her instructions attentively. As the day progressed, our communication got more relaxed. She stopped being so aggressive and demanding with me and began to become somewhat personable. I assumed her attitude had changed because it was near the end of her shift and she was about to go home for the day.

As we arrived at the Bellstand, another Bellman appeared to start his shift. "Oh! Shamar, let me introduce you to Gene Little. He's the mid-day Bellman who will continue training you after I leave." We made a quick greeting and Precious went to clock out for the day. Gene said, "Well I see you got schooled today by Miss Thing." Gene told me to follow him, while he led me to the luggage room where the guests' property was stored and went on to explain that we issued tickets to guests for their things.

Gene showed me all the exits of the hotel in case of an emergency and even took me on a tour of the employee's café. "Now Shamar," he said, "let me show you another set of elevators in case you get real busy and need to get an impatient guest to his room. We have the busiest hotel in the city as well as the most demanding guests you will ever encounter. Our hotel spoils our guests and they know it." At this point, I was totally impressed with Gene's concern about my knowledge of the job. He was patient and polite toward me.

After taking my lunch, I rejoined Gene back at the Bellstand. He was in the process of going to check a guest out of his room and told me to hurry and follow him. We quickly caught the elevator and he continued explaining how things were done. Gene was precise with every direction he gave. He was very detail-oriented and followed every rule by the book. Upon arrival at the guest's room, I stayed politely at the door to observe. The guest made it clear to Gene that he wanted his luggage stored until he finished his meeting.

Gene assured the guest that his luggage will be properly stored and to give his room number when he came to claim it. As he finished loading the cart, the guest handed Gene a fifty-dollar bill. I began to get excited and was anxious for him to leave the room. While traveling back to the lobby of the hotel, Gene did not utter a word about the large tip he had just received. I became disillusioned because I just knew he would share it with me.

However, this was not the case and I could not abstain from asking him about the situation. I thought back to earlier when I worked with Precious. She hadn't shared one dollar with me, although I assisted in loading and unloading guest's luggage with her. So I rationalized that since this was my first day I had to accept the rules that were in place. My only comfort was that I knew I had two more days left for training and then I would be on my own. It was just a thrill to see how much money the Bellman could make in one day.

While posted up at the Bellstand, the Front Check-in Counter was extremely busy. Another Bellman came on duty and immediately introduced himself to me. "Hello, Shamar, I'm Rickey. Or you can call me Rick, everyone one else does. I just got through talking to Mr. Gentry and he told me to make you comfortable on your first day. How did you like working with Precious and Gene?" I said, "Well, Precious was somewhat impatient with me, but Gene was more detailed on how things operate around here. I learned a lot from him."

"Don't let Gene fool you man," Rickey responded. "He's a greedy mother-fucker and I hate him." I was taken aback. The only thing I could do was listen to what he had to say about his co-workers.

Now at this moment, Gene walked up and the two greeted each other because they work the same shift. I was perplexed at this situation because I didn't know who I would be finishing my day with. The only thing I knew for sure was that my shift would be ending in two hours and it didn't really matter how it was. Anyway, things worked out because I alternated between the two and learned a lot about their personalities and how they work with guests.

As I was leaving the hotel after my first shift, I encountered Mr. Gentry. "Hey, Shamar," he said. "How was your first day? I meant to come by to check on you but I was in meetings all day. How did you like working with the other Bellmen? Do you think you're cut out to be one?"

I didn't think he would ask me three questions at once, but I answered the same way he asked. "My first day was adventurous," I said. "And all the Bellmen I worked with were very informative and I'm going to love being a Guest Service Aide." He said, "That's great!" and welcomed me aboard.

The next two days of training went very well. Learning to be a Bellman was as delightful as being a Diplomat.

The uniforms we wore were highlighted with gold stitching and large brass buttons. Our royal presentation made guests feel like they were at a Queen's Court. After meeting all the staff I was working with, I became confident that this would be the last job I would hold in life. I was looking forward to the next day when I would be working independently.

It's On!

My impression of the hotel industry was that it was a place of relief, a place to relax and get pampered. Imagine leaving home for a few days to relieve yourself of all the anxiety of household chores. Cutting the grass, fixing dinner, cleaning the house, seeing the kids off to school, you name it – it's your life in a cycle. It doesn't get any better if you live in solitude without the comfort of a significant other. Your social life is in peril of loneliness without an end.

But isn't it great when the CEO of your company announces that the entire staff will be attending a conference at one of the prestigious hotels in the Midwest? And that you'll be traveling with all expenses paid by your company, including meals and hotel amenities? The thought of taking just enough cash to enjoy yourself only comes around when an occasion like this arises. Normally when you take a trip or vacation, it's expensive. That is the time when you clean out your savings or dip into your 401K to make ends meet. But now, a free trip!! You have to thank GOD for that!

On my first day working alone, a stream of conventioneers began filling the lobby to check in. We had reservations for one thousand guests. A five-day stay assured me that tips would be great. Although I was somewhat nervous, I knew my first approach had to be flawless, not lacking in any confidence. I had to be attentive of any request made of me and be very responsive. I became relaxed when I thought of the times when my charm attracted people to me. I was always held to high standards while engaged in social activities. So why not apply the same attitude here?

As I stood at the Bellstand awaiting my turn to take the next guest to their room, a lady approached me. "Sir, are you a Bellman?" she asked.

"Yes, ma'am," I responded. "I'm Shamar. Welcome to The Grandeur Hotel. May I assist you?" Little did I know that this lady had already checked in and had her room key. I didn't notice any luggage so I looked around to see if someone had brought her luggage in without me noticing it.

"Thanks for asking," the guest said. "If you don't mind, sir, I need you to do me a favor. Since it was so busy out front when I drove up, I self-parked my vehicle in the hotel garage and left all my luggage in the trunk. I am driving a grey Lexus® and it's parked on the green level. Here are my keys and my plates read 'SPOILED.' If you don't mind, sir, I would appreciate it if you would bring my luggage to room 1812."

Although the garage was located one block from the hotel, I didn't hesitate to respond. "Ma'am, don't you worry. I would be delighted to get your luggage and bring it to your room."

I hurried to retrieve a bell cart and proceeded to the hotel garage. As I was leaving, Precious came from behind me and gave me a hard slap on my ass. I was startled but the only words she uttered were, "Get that money, boy." I continued on my journey but couldn't help to think about why they called her Miss Thing. As I looked back at her, she had her bell jacket pulled over her waist adjusting her pants. Her curved physique was alluring, but I ignored her.

My only focus was to get this guest's luggage to the guest's room as soon as possible. I encountered Gene in the driveway without a bell cart, and he immediately tried to take mine and give me this sermon about how he had more seniority than me and that I needed to find another cart. I thought of Rickey telling me that Gene was an asshole – which he was demonstrating at this point. With this thought, I snatched my cart back and continued with my objective.

These distractions made me very upset on my first day working alone. About twenty minutes had expired before I finally arrived at room 1812 with the luggage. This was when I composed myself and posted a big smile on my face before knocking. I repeatedly knocked at the room door, but there was no response. I didn't know if the guest had arrived or had she left out of disappointment on my delay.

After several knocks, I reluctantly put my master key into the lock, thinking that I'd be leaving this luggage in the room without receiving a tip. This was a frustrating thought because I had done a lot of labor and traveling for this guest. As I entered the room, the guest surprised me by emerging from the shower with only a towel pressed against her breast and everything else was visible. I dumbly stood there in shock and apologized as I began to explain to her that I knocked several times without a response.

I was surprised when she didn't seem to be upset or uncomfortable about me seeing her in the nude. Instead, she apologized to me for not hearing my knocks at the door. She continued to put the guest robe on while instructing as to where to unload her luggage. I pilfered a glance at her while she retrieved some cash out of her purse and placed it in my hand. She said, "Thank you, Shamar. You're a great Bellman and I appreciate you going all the way to the garage to get my luggage." I thanked her graciously for the twenty-five dollar tip and left her room.

While traveling the long corridor back to the elevator, I crossed paths with another Bellman who I hadn't yet met. He was in a hurry with a cart full of luggage, so we briefly introduced ourselves without interrupting the rhythm of our steps. His name was Charles.

When I got back to the lobby, it was extremely busy. Mr. Gentry and two other Managers were directing all movements of visitors, guests, and doormen, and were assigning destinations to the bellmen. "Shamar, take this cart to room 1536. The guest has been waiting 10 minutes. Hurry!" Mr. Gentry said. I grabbed the cart and was on my way.

We had ten Front Desk Clerks on duty that day, along with their Supervisors, and all the lines were full of guests checking in and out of the hotel. The lobby had a circus atmosphere and I had to dodge the maze of people while pulling at least three hundred pounds of luggage: stressed out and tired was an understatement of how I felt mid-way through the day. I must have taken one hundred guests to their rooms at this point, but I wasn't complaining because my pockets were full of cash from the tips.

The day was moving so swiftly that a lunch break did not come to my mind. However, while escorting another guest to their room, Mr. Gentry approached me. "Shamar, after you take your guest to their room, come back to the office. I ordered pizza for everybody. I know you guys been running all day, so take a break. And by the way, I'm proud of the job you're doing on your first day alone. Your style of greeting the guests is very personable and charming, which makes our hotel shine in a good light." I said, "Thank you, Mr. Gentry, for your compliment. That's what I'm here for, to serve the guests."

As I made my way to room 1753, I noticed through my peripheral vision that Gene was giving Mr. Gentry a disgusted, jealous look. You see, Gene's attitude with the guests was to get their luggage, ask them for their room number, and then tell them to follow him. He barely talked to them as he took them to their rooms. His personality was cut and dry.

The guest I was taking to room 1753 was Dr. Cook. He noticed Gene's expression, too. He said, "Shamar, I must agree with your boss. You do have a pleasant personality, but what's wrong with your co-worker? He appeared to be upset at your conversation with him. How long have you two been working together?"

"Dr. Cook," I said, "He's been working here ten years and I've only been working here three days." At this point, I wanted the conversation to end about Gene's attitude because I knew he was an ass. Anyway, I don't believe in speaking bad about anyone. I just wanted to mind my own business and not let anyone's personal feelings about me interfere with my goal to satisfy the guests. I knew that if I got caught up in trivial episodes I would not be focused on the plan I had set for myself. So after I unloaded Dr. Cook's luggage in his room I asked if there was anything else I could do for him. "Yes, could you get me some ice?" he asked. "I need to make a nice drink."

I proceeded with his request and when I return he thanked me and handed me a $20 tip.

As I was leaving Dr. Cook's room, I received a call on my radio. "Hello, Shamar this is Precious. Please answer." I immediately responded. "Hi, Precious, can I help you?" The radio went blank without a response, so I went on down to the lobby, confused. When I arrived in the lobby I began looking for her, but she was nowhere in sight. When I saw Rick coming out of the bell closet and asked him if he had seen her, his response was that he saw her go into the office. Good, I thought because I knew that's where the pizza was. I thought about how considerate Mr. Gentry was in thinking about us not having lunch all day.

As I opened the office door, there was Precious with her jaws opened, ready to sink her teeth into a nice slice of pizza. She looked at me and said, "Oh, Shamar, I just tried calling you to let you know that all the pizza was almost gone, but I was able to secure you a few pieces, baby. Come over here and sit next to me." I was surprised because Precious had always given me a hard time since my first day of training. I became forgiving of her stern projection of dominance.

I took my seat next to her and began eating my food when she struck up a flirtatious conversation. She started telling me a sad story about her life. Precious ("Miss Thing") was a forty-year-old woman who had been married to her childhood sweetheart, but got divorced after twenty years and three kids. After being happily married all that time her husband had begun abusing crack cocaine, which destroyed their relationship. Now she found it hard to find a good man who was willing to share quality time.

Her desire to find another man in her life was trivial to me. But before we departed, she did make it known that she admired me and would like to spend more time together to get acquainted. I wasn't too excited about this because I didn't have affairs with co-workers; it gets out of control and feelings get hurt. But now it was time to get back to work. Our shift was almost over and I was anxious to get back to making tips. However, I couldn't help thinking how desirable Precious was and that maybe I could hit it once.

Servicing

The simplicity of being a Bellman was overshadowed by the hard work of lifting heavy luggage and pulling loaded carts. This is compounded by having to travel through a two thousand-room hotel with twin towers. The Grandeur was one of two five-star-rated hotels in the area. This was evidence of all the amenities we provided guests.

One of the greatest amenities was that we provided free internet to guests' rooms. This was why we got a lot of Fortune 500 companies to hold their conferences here. The hotel provided other services, too, such as the concierge club lounge where preferred guests could unwind and grab a bite to eat at no charge. There was even a large fitness center comparable to Bally's Spa. The hotel was breathtaking and standing in the lobby servicing guests was a privilege. I felt thrilled to greet people who appreciated my service.

I was just stepping off the elevator into the lobby when the phone rang at the Bell Stand. I rushed to answer it. "Hello, this is the Bell Stand, Shamar speaking. May I help you?" The voice on the other end responded, "This is Ms. D in room 1812. Will you please send a Bellman to my room to pick up my laundry? I'm busy on my computer and don't have time to bring it down."

Now it is customary for guests to bring their own laundry down to the Bell Stand before 9 AM. That's the time the outside laundry service comes to the hotel and pick up their dry-cleaning. Ms. D was six hours late and it was time for me to get off.

However, I said, "Yes, Ms. D, I'll be delighted to pick up your laundry, and I'm on my way." But I was frustrated because I was about to end my day and there were no other Bellmen around. As I proceeded to her room, I realized that this was the guest who I caught coming out of the shower. I must say that the frustration went away immediately because she had given me a fat tip earlier.

When I got to room 1812, the door was open and Miss D was just putting her clothes in the laundry bag. "Oh, Shamar," she said. "I see you're still here. Thank you very much for picking up my laundry. Is there any way I can get it back by 6 PM? I have a dinner I must attend and I need this suit. I know it's late but if you could get this done for me I will take good care of you." This was a request that I could not refuse. The problem was that I would have to find a cleaners open that would have the time to do it. I assured Ms. D that I would do my best but couldn't promise her anything.

So I grabbed the bag and hurried off to find a cleaner that had their steam up. I knew that I had frequented one that was one block from the hotel, so I rushed there and the owner reluctantly accepted my plea to have Miss D's clothes done in one hour. Again, I had to rush back to the hotel because it was time for me to clock out. It took about 40 minutes to clock out and change clothes. Then I ran back to the cleaners and Mr. Lee was about to leave.

Mr. Lee was a Korean immigrant and was very money-hungry. I knew I was going to be taxed very hard for the special service. As I entered the cleaners he began telling me how he had to turn his steam back on and pay his help more money to stay over and clean my clothes. After hearing him complain I just grabbed my ass and asked what my bill was. To my surprise, he gave me a break and only charged me $25. I was elated. "Thank you Mr. Lee," I said. I paid him and left with Miss D's clothes on time.

It was 5 PM when I stepped back into the hotel lobby. While catching the elevator back to room 1812, who was getting off but Gene. He said, "Oh, Shamar, I thought you were already gone for the day. What are you doing with that laundry? There wasn't any laundry left in the Bell Closet. Are you doing special duties for a guest?" I hurried on the waiting elevator and didn't answer him at all. I just waved my hand.

When I arrived at Ms. D's room I sprayed myself with the sample bottle of cologne I always carry with me. She was a beautiful woman and I could not help but think of that naked body I had seen earlier that day. Keep in mind that she acted as if I wasn't present when I entered her room. As I knocked on her door, she answered, "Who's there?" "This is Shamar, the Bellman, with your laundry," I said. While waiting for her to open the door I looked down the corridor and noticed Gene peeping around the corner at me. He was spying on me!

The door opened and I entered the room anyway. I presented Ms. D with her laundry and explained how I almost wasn't able to accomplish this goal due to how late I had gotten it. She told me to have a seat until she finished her conversation on the phone.

So I sat down, knowing that the service I had provided her with would be well rewarded. I assumed this because she could have simply taken her clothes and sent me on. As I sat there watching her pace about the room talking on the phone, I began to get nervous. I realized that I was off the clock and had no business sitting in a guest's room when I should have been out of the hotel. If security knew this, or Mr. Gentry, I was sure I would lose my job.

This is when I motioned to the door indicating to Ms. D that I had to leave. She finished her conversation and said, "I'm sorry, Shamar, to keep you waiting, but I didn't want you to leave without paying you. Now tell me, how much do I owe you for this considerate service you provided me? You really didn't have to go out your way to do this and I'm grateful." I was lost for words on this compliment, so I just told her to give me whatever she thought it would was worth. She gave me a big smile and handed me a one hundred dollar bill.

I graciously thanked Ms. D and as I began to exit the door, she asked me where was a nice place she could have a cocktail after dinner. I told her that the hotel had a nice bar located on the other side of the Concierge Stand. She responded, "Now Shamar, I've been in your bar before and it's not the place I would like to be to unwind. Tell me, where can I go to hear some music and dance?" This response surprised me. I immediately told her that I sometimes stopped at Club Elite after work for happy hour. I told her that after 8:00 PM the DJ starts playing music until closing time. I gave her the location of the club, which was only two blocks away from the hotel. You see, the hotel was located in the downtown business district of the city. This was a playground for all of the sports events, concerts, tourist attractions, you name it – everyone of elite status came to play around the hotel. When I gave her this information, she gave me an approving smile and I left the room.

When I got off the elevator, I saw Gene whispering to one of the Managers of the hotel, so I jetted out the side door so he couldn't see me. I knew he had followed me to Ms. D's room and assumed that he was telling the Manager he saw me enter a guest's room when I was supposed to be off work. The thought of this had me in a dilemma. I didn't know what to expect when I returned to work the next day. I knew I had to come up with a legitimate reason for why I was in Ms D's room.

Anyway, I scrubbed the thought from my mind and headed home with the thought of Ms. D going to Club Elite tonight. It was 6:00 PM when I thought of her being at the dinner she had to attend. I imagined that un-scarred tan body I saw earlier in the day. It was alluring for me to fantasize how erotic I could be with her. However, I knew that was impossible. I could not involve myself with the guests of the hotel. But, she gave me the impression that she would like to see me there.

I finally decided I was going to Club Elite that evening. It was a hard decision to make because I was exhausted from all the traveling I did servicing the guests and I wondered about Gene. The only thing that relaxed my mind was when I sat on my bed and counted the tips for the day. My enthusiasm came up quick when I summed up $726. I had never before made that kind of money in one day. It didn't even take that much money to raise me.

My motivation got stronger when I thought about Ms. D making an appearance at Club Elite after her dinner engagement. I could not get the thought of that woman off my mind. It wasn't that I was a freak; it was the alluring personality she possessed. With these thoughts in mind, I immediately ran to the shower to freshen up. Even if she didn't show up, I'd have fun because there were always good pickings at Club Elite.

The evening was perfect. I felt rejuvenated after arriving at the club in my stylish attire. The atmosphere was laced with some of the most beautiful women in the city. It got better after I had a few cocktails and was able to buy drinks for a couple of coworkers who stopped in after work. I kept my eyes at the entrance anticipating Ms. D's arrival, but to no avail. After a couple of hours, Rick approached me. "Hey, Shamar, I didn't know you were here. Man, I looked all over the hotel for you today."

I said, "Well, here I am now, man. What's up?" He said, "I told you to watch out for that asshole, Gene. He told the night manager, Mr. Gerritzen, that after you had clocked out for the day, he saw you take a change of clothes to a guest room and stay there for an hour."

After hearing this, I sunk my head in my hands and said, "Lord, help me…" He continued to tell me how bewildered Mr.

Gerritzen was looking as Gene told him how I was breaking hotel rules by staying in the room of a hotel guest.

When we ended our conversation, my evening was over. There was no enjoyment in my presence at the Club at this point, so I immediately left for home. I couldn't sleep after hearing the story about Gene's disloyalty to me. I was distraught. This was the time I had to show the other side of my personality – the side that doesn't let me get hurt. This hotel was going to be my future and nobody was going to interfere with that.

New Attitude

Another day. Another dollar. This was my only thought as I entered the hotel's locker room to get ready to start work. I didn't let the previous day's activity ruin my attitude. I concluded that I hadn't done anything wrong or against hotel policy because our mission as hotel employees was to satisfy our guests by any means necessary. This is what I was told during my orientation and I swore to do this.

I always arrived thirty minutes early to any job. This gives me time to grab something to eat and relax. As I entered our spacious employee café, I noticed Mr. Gentry at a table having coffee and a roll. We locked eyes with one another and he motioned for me to come join him at his table. That was the slowest walk I had since starting at The Grandeur.

I sat down with the man who I respected and owed great gratitude. He said, "Good morning, Shamar. We have another busy day ahead and I'm glad you are here. We have a group of doctors checking into the hotel and they are very observant of the services we provide them. We strive very hard to meet their every need, so be attentive at all times to whatever they request of you. Sometimes they demand too much, but if you are confronted with request you can't handle, please call me." I just responded that I would do my best.

After my response, Mr. Gentry stood and exited the café in the direction of the lobby. I was relieved that he didn't mention the episode that Gene had exposed and I sighed in relief. Once again, I knew it was going to be a challenging day because I was a new Bellman and all eyes were going to be on me.

My inspiration came back when I arrived in the lobby and saw it filled with guests trying to check into the hotel. Precious zoomed past me with a loaded cart of luggage and a big smile on her face. She said, "Shamar, you need to hurry up and get busy. These doctors are tipping good." I had to give her credit – she was a hustler. No other Bellman could compare to her speed in delivering the guests to their rooms. This made her very prosperous. Guests felt obligated to tip her handsomely since she was a female lifting their heavy bags. After leaving a room, she would wave her tips in your face.

I noticed Gene loading a cart and the guest was hurrying him along. It appeared that the guest was anxious to get to his room. I heard him say, "Bellman, I'll meet you in my room. I'm running late for my conference and I need to shower and change clothes. Hurry, please!!" As he got into the elevator, Gene left his cart unattended and went into the Bell Closet. This was my chance to get revenge for the lies he told. I immediately grabbed his cart and took it outside the hotel where the Doorman could not see it.

I knew that if anyone saw me, I would lose my job. Then a thought came to my mind – there were security cameras posted all over the hotel lobby. Damn! My every move was recorded. Not only was I nervous, I panicked at the realization of the mistake I had made. As I thought to retrieve the cart, I saw Gene running around the lobby frantically looking for his cart. He was asking everyone in his sight had they seen it. This was getting hilarious and I was enjoying every minute of his despair. I just stood back by the concierge desk, watching every move he made. I knew it would not be long before the guest began calling the front desk inquiring after his luggage. Gene noticed me and said, "Shamar, did you see the luggage cart I sat in front of you when you arrived in the lobby?" I knew at that moment he was trying to use me as a scapegoat, so I calmly told him, "Sorry, man, I didn't see you with a cart. I was helping a guest. Maybe it was Rick you saw."

Gene gave me a puzzled look, as though he wasn't sure what he had done with his cart. I immediately walked toward the Bell Stand where Mr. Gentry was talking on the phone. He was speaking with the guest whom Gene was supposed to deliver his luggage to and I could hear him screaming at Mr. Gentry about how he'd been waiting for thirty minutes. Mr. Gentry assured the guest it would be there soon and he hung up the phone very hard out of disgust.

"Shamar, where's Gene?" he asked. "I hope he is on his way to room 2012 with the guest's luggage." I told Mr. Gentry that I saw Gene catch the elevator going upstairs and didn't see him pulling a cart. Little did Gene know that the luggage was sitting outside the hotel, compliments of me. I assumed that Gene was on his way to the guest's room to see if he had taken up his own luggage. Ten minutes later, he came back looking as bewildered as before. Mr. Gentry asked him what was going on.

At this time, I could not help but go outside so I could get off a big laugh. The Doorman approached me while I was outside; his name was Phil. "What's up Shamar?" he asked. "Why are you running out of the hotel laughing? Tell me what's funny?" I could not disclose the prank I had pulled on Gene because there could have been retribution, so I told him that Precious had told me a joke about the date she had last night.

He said, "Look, man, you can't fool me. I saw everything that just happened. I saw you pull the cart out here and hide it. I knew Gene was looking for it and probably still is, but you don't have to worry about me saying a thing about it, he's not my favorite person either. The only thing you better worry about is that they didn't look at the cameras to see where it went." After listening to Phil, I immediately pulled the cart back into the lobby and left it where Gene would see it.

I couldn't wait around to see the aftermath of Gene's problem. The only thing I was concerned about was that Phil wouldn't tell a soul about what I had done. If that cat was let out the bag, I would be a goner.

The rest of that day, it was business as usual, grabbing luggage and taking my guests to their rooms. Suddenly, Precious approached me and asked for my assistance with two heavy carts she had to deliver. I saw that she was barely able to pull one of them. It wasn't unusual for us to take two carts up at once, but when they are loaded to the max, it becomes impossible.

I told her I would be glad to help, but I stressed that she must split whatever gratuity received for her service with me. She said she didn't have a problem with that and we proceeded. While going to the room, Precious reminded me of the conversation we had about us going out together when we got off work. The guest hadn't arrived to the room so Precious used her key to enter. As we started unloading the luggage, she suddenly grabbed me and stuck her tongue down my mouth out of pure ecstasy. I could not help but oblige this temptation.

My feelings were overcome by rubbing my hands slowly around her large round ass, which made her reciprocate. As we indulged each other with passionate kisses, an erection came over me and suddenly the guest tried to enter the room. We quickly pulled apart and greeted the guest as he entered. He gave us a suspicious look as though he knew what we were doing. He said, "Oh! Did I interrupt you two? I really appreciate your service and I know I had a lot of shit, so here you go." He gave Precious and me twenty dollars each and we exited the room.

As we were going down the corridor, the guest stuck his head outside his room and said, "Hey, guys, you're welcome to come back up and finish your business, I won't say a word if I can participate." It surprised the shit out of me when Precious turned around and said, "I'll be glad to come back up but it's going to cost you more than twenty dollars." I thought I would die after that statement. Not only did she betray herself as a whore, but she was an employee of the hotel. The guest responded, "Well you know where I'm at."

While waiting for the elevator to go back to the lobby, Precious asked me if I wanted to finish where we left off. She caught me off-guard with that question. As much as I wanted to say yes, I knew we were at work and it didn't mix with fucking. I guessed this is why she was called "Miss Thing." However, I responded by saying, "Yes, let's do it, baby." She gave me a smirk and told me to follow her. She guided me to the housekeeping room and instructed me to put both our carts inside there.

I felt somewhat foolish because I was letting Precious dominate my sense of reasoning and I knew that if we were caught it would be the end of our jobs. I couldn't believe I was letting this feeling of sexual desire overrule my sense of reasoning. I could not help but think about the guest we had just left in room 1612 who also desired Precious. As beautiful as she was, it wasn't hard for any man to get weak with lust for her. Her plan was for us to use an unoccupied guest room, which she used her passkey to enter, for our finale. She said, "Come on, boy, let me give you some of this young coochie."

At this point, I realized I didn't have any protection and there was no way I was going to have sex without one. Precious reassured me that she was always prepared for this situation and pulled out a fresh box of Trojans. This was very discouraging for me. My perception of her sexuality changed immediately: the alluring sexiness she exuded was replaced with a thought of slutness. I guess it was her domineering approach that changed my mind, and after all, I was at work on hotel property.

You see, I was not a young man anymore and I had to think of my future. Getting a job like this was a blessing that I could not ignore. It took me back to the day I got on my knees in front of The Grandeur and prayed to the Lord that he bless me with this job. We are challenged every day with temptation that could be detrimental to our lives. This situation would have been detrimental for me because I finally had security. I thought, where else could I find a job at the age of 56 that provides health benefits? I didn't have to think anymore, so I kindly rejected Precious and left the room.

Back in the lobby, I noticed that Precious did not come downstairs. This was confusing because all the Bellmen were very busy. It was not like her to miss any traffic in the hotel. Guests were in a frenzy trying to check in and get to their meetings. As I emerged from the Bell Closet, I noticed Dr. Cook, who had been checked in for two days. He was moving very slowly and his eyes seemed dazed. There was a stumble in his step as though he was about to fall. I immediately rushed over and grabbed his arm.

At this point, he lost his balance so I had to sit him on a Bell Cart. I looked around for help and noticed Precious rushing over. All of a sudden, there was a panic in the lobby. Several managers and guests surrounded Dr. Cook trying to see what was wrong. Most of guests checking in were doctors and he had the best of care. After all the excitement was over, Dr. Cook appeared to be alright. He was a premier guest of the hotel because he organized this big conference every year that yielded large revenue for the hotel.

In the crowd I saw the guest from room 1812 (SPOILED), Ms. D, giving me a gesture to come over to her. As I approached her she said, "Shamar, will you please go down to the FedEx® Store and pick up some packages for me and deliver them to my room? They were too heavy for me to carry."

I told her that I would be delighted and proceeded to grant her request. As I was leaving the lobby, Precious angrily approached me and said, "That was some punk shit you pulled on me upstairs. You should have told me you were scared of pussy. Why didn't you just let me know you weren't interested?"

I responded, "Listen, baby, I got caught up in the heat of passion with you. You are a beautiful and sexy woman but I don't get sexually involved with my coworkers. I apologize for leading you on, but I can't afford to lose my job over some sex. Now if you don't mind, I have to get down to the FedEx® Store." I left her staring at me with a hateful frown. I didn't give a damn because I had a task to perform and the guests were watching.

I eagerly retrieved the packages for Ms. D and rushed to her room. Upon my arrival, she began asking me about the incident with Precious. She said she had overheard our conversation and asked if she was my girlfriend. I was embarrassed by the whole situation, especially with her knowing what had transpired between us. I told Ms. D that she was not my woman and that I was trying to deter her advances.

I began to wonder why Ms. D was being so personable. She began to tell me how she had just been divorced from her husband of thirty years. He left her for a woman twenty years her junior, with whom he'd had a child. She continued to tell me how long it had taken for her to find a man she could be intimate with. "Shamar," she said, "I wasn't trying to be nosy but I kind of sympathize with the lady you had this discussion with. She's probably lonely like I am. A woman needs some compassion in her life," she said.

This conversation left me amazed because the only thing I was trying to do was deliver her package and get a big tip. I wasn't expecting to hear the sob story of her tormented marriage. As I stood there waiting for my tip, she broke down crying. I didn't know if I should console her or walk my ass out her room. But a feeling of compassion came over me because I knew women were very sensitive, so I embraced Ms. D and she gently laid her head on my shoulder. After a quiet, somber moment, Ms. D collected herself and grabbed her purse. She reached inside and handed me a fifty-dollar bill.

She said, "Shamar , I'm so sorry that I brought this on you – thanks for picking up my package and listening to my sad life. I don't know what happened to me, but I'm sorry." After receiving the $50 tip, she could have cried a river. However, I thanked her and assured her that I understood her feelings and to let me know if I could do anything else. As I was about to leave her room, she asked me what time I was getting off work. I told her that I would be leaving at 3:30. She asked if I would give her a call before I left and I said I would.

When I got back to the lobby, as usual, it was busy. I was very energetic and felt very good about myself. I had not yet crossed the line of respect for other people's feelings and I hadn't succumbed to the sexual advances of Precious, nor did I take advantage of Ms. D's vulnerability. As I approached the Bell Stand, one of the valet guys waved me to the Bell Closet. Inside, he informed me that a guest needed his luggage unloaded from his vehicle and that the Doorman was not available. I immediately grabbed a cart and proceeded to unload the guest's luggage. I told the guest to go inside and check in and that I'd follow behind him.

At this time, Mr. Gerritzen was coming on duty. We greeted each other and Mr. Gerritzen said, "Oh, Shamar, later on when we're not so busy, I would like to speak with you." This threw me for a loop because I couldn't figure out why he needed to speak with me. Anyway, I continued to bring the cart to the Check-in Desk and wait for the guest. On the way up to his room, the guest asked if I was a new Bellman and I told him that I was. He explained that he had been coming to the hotel for a long time and loved our service.

Things Getting Thick

In the guest's room, we made a quick introduction and I assured him that I would be at his service if he needed me for anything. He acknowledged my politeness and tipped me handsomely. As I returned to the lobby, Mr. Gerritzen summoned me to his office and asked me about staying in Ms. D's room after work.

When I didn't respond, Mr. Gerritzen said, "Look, Shamar, let me explain what's going on. Gene approached me the other day and he told me saw you carrying your clothes into a guest's room and that you stayed an hour. Employees are not supposed to have personal relationships with the guests. For example, if you have a problem with a guest, the guest could become angry with you and complain that you harassed them. You see, Shamar, this opens the hotel up for lawsuits. This action is cause for immediate dismissal, so please give me your explanation."

All the time he was speaking, I was paying close attention to his demeanor and body language. My response would depend on if I felt he believed Gene or not. To my surprise, he didn't seem angry and came across with a doubtful attitude about the whole situation. He was smiling as he spoke, which told me I had a chance to sway his thoughts.

"Now Shamar," he said, "I'm not taking sides, and I know Gene doesn't get along with other employees well, but did you personally have a problem with him?"

He didn't know he had opened the door for me to get out of this by asking that question. My response was that Gene was very aggressive while training me for the job. I explained there were several incidents where he wouldn't let me take a guest up to their room. I told him that Gene had hogged me out of several tips that were for me. I really got his attention when I told him that a guest had called the Bell Stand and requested my service, and instead of informing me, Gene went up himself. Mr. Gerritzen wasn't thrilled by my accusations.

This is when I explained the incident in Ms. D's room. I said, "Mr. Gerritzen, you know I'm new on this job. The guest in room 1812 requested that I take some last-minute laundry to be cleaned, so I obliged. Gene saw me delivering her laundry back to her room after I picked it up from the cleaners down the street. I didn't have to do this at all because I was off work, but the motto of the hotel is to service our guest to the best of our ability – and I did this. As far as being in her room for an hour, that is a damn lie. The guest was on the phone when I arrived and she told me to wait for my tip."

At this point Mr. Gerritzen interjected and told me he had heard enough. He said I was free to go and not to mention this stupid shit to anyone. As I left his office, I was looking for Gene so I could curse his ass out but he had left for the day. With relief, I realized it was about time for me to get off work and I had told Mrs. D that I would give her a call before I left. I was hesitant to do so, because all this drama was because of her. But I put this aside and called her room.

While getting ready to call Mrs. D's room, the guest I had just taken up before all this started came over to the Bell Stand. I had gotten into the habit of remembering room numbers instead of names, which was a bad practice. Putting faces with room numbers gave me the advantage to remember the best tippers. However, guests prefer that you call them by name. Anyway, the guest told me his name was John Cook and wanted to know the direction to Club Elite. After giving him instructions, I proceeded to call Ms. D's room.

I couldn't imagine why she wanted me to call her before I got off work. Although I was puzzled, the thought was overshadowed by her generosity. She told me she was overwhelmed with the desire for some companionship for the evening. She went on to stress how lonely she'd been for over a year and found it difficult to approach a man. This was a very perplexing request for me because I couldn't think of anyone I could hook her up with. All my friends were married, so I offered myself as a date.

Satisfying Our Guests

Although I was just disciplined by Mr. Gerritzen, I felt a sympathetic obligation to Ms. D's position. Here was a sexy middle-aged woman who had experienced a tragedy in her marriage. Not a tragedy where there was death or injury, but where a heart was broken that hadn't had the chance to heal. I realized that the hotel rules didn't allow employees to get personally involved with guests, but this was a situation where I could satisfy and give comfort to a lonely soul. So I did not feel guilty; I was only giving moral support to someone who needed it.

After meeting Ms. D at a restaurant close to the hotel, her self-esteem seemed to lift. She was in a joyous and happy mood. However, as the end of our encounter neared, she became sad again. We had joked and laughed all through dinner and her demeanor caught me by surprise. She explained that being in my company had been the best time she had spent with a man in years. Her life had been work and raising her family without the enjoyment of a social life. We ended our evening with a big caress and parted ways.

While Ms. D walked back to the hotel, I decided not to go straight home – it was happy hour at Club Elite and I thought I would drop in there. I had to have a drink after leaving a woman who I had seen nude and who was in a very vulnerable state where she could have easily been open to having sex. It was obvious to me that this was Ms. D's desire. But I had to get that thought off my mind because I knew that action could have backfired on me. I must admit that a man's instinct often takes over rational thinking.

Anyway, I arrived at Club Elite to an ecstatic after-work crowd. It was happy hour and the drinks were two-for-one. The tables were full of empty glasses and the patrons were partying on the dance floor. I immediately fell into the groove and ordered my favorite cocktail. As I was at the door bouncing to the beat of the DJ, the bartender brought me another round of drinks that I had not ordered. He said that the guy in the gray suit had bought me a drink. When I glanced over at the bar, it was the guest, John Cook. When I thanked him, his response was, "Let me tell you something, Shamar: you are the best Bellman I ever met. Your attire and personality really make you stand out. The aroma of your cologne is pleasant and alluring. Can I ask, are you married, Shamar?" The first thing that came to mind after his compliments was that this motherfucker is gay. I gave him a disappointing stare that he could have interpreted as a sign of anger. I assumed he was gay when I first took him to his room because of his proper accent.

Being the professional person I was, I could not give him a negative response nor let him know that I objected to his curiosity in my personal life. I realized that my objective was to make the entire guest that I serviced feel comfortable and admirable towards me. This is how you are rewarded with large tips; a person must like you. Anyway, I thanked John for the drink and the compliment he gave me. I did tell him that I wasn't married but I had a fiancé. John and I continued to have conversation throughout the evening and even got drunk together.

It was almost 9 o'clock and happy hour was about to end when to my surprise Mrs. D stepped into the club. I almost didn't recognize her because she looked so fabulous. She strutted in looking like a model out of Vogue magazine. She wore a fresh facade of makeup on and was wearing a stunning strapless red mini dress. Every man at club was turning their heads to pilfer a glance at her curvaceous physique. It appeared to me that she was on a mission to be recognized for the alluring beauty she possessed. I must admit I got a chubby imaging what was under that skirt.

This was the guest who I had just had dinner with a couple of hours ago. She didn't look this appetizing earlier. I wrestled with the thought of male egotism for sex or rationalization of being a gentleman and an employee of the hotel. I put all thoughts aside and went with my male instinct, and approached her with the flirtatious desire she was seeking. "Hello Mrs. D, it's nice seeing you again. Come on, let's dance." I said. I grabbed her hand and led her to the dance floor. We both explored each other out of ecstasy; dancing on a slow jam.

Well, the evening was fun and it was time to go home. I knew I had to go to work the next morning, so I departed early. I enjoyed the evening with Mrs. D and John. The last comment from Mrs. D was that she was checking out of the hotel the next day.

The next day, when I arrived at work, there was a message left at the Bell Stand for me to pick up the guest luggage in room 1812 at 10 o'clock. I knew it was a big checkout because one of the conferences was ending and we were going to be very busy.

As we started getting calls for luggage pickups, my focus was on the Valet guys taking carts out to the guest's vehicles and cabs. Sometimes when you go to a guest's room, they request that you take their luggage down to the lobby and they will be there shortly. While waiting for the guest to arrive, you'll get a call from another guest requesting service. The luggage of the guest that you are waiting for is unattended and the valet guy takes the luggage out when the guest appears. This is called stealing because the Bellman misses a tip. I cannot blame the valet – he's just trying to make some money like me.

I do my best to get a tip before I leave the room. I let the guest know that I will be leaving his luggage at the Bell Stand because we're so busy that I may have to leave before he arrives to the lobby. I assure him that I will have someone watching his luggage. Usually the guest would be considerate enough to go ahead and tip you then. It helps a lot if you were the Bellman who checked him or her in. That is one strategy I use. Another one is that I tell the guest he can call valet service and have his car brought in front of the hotel so I can load him up and be ready to go.

This service often guarantees a hefty tip because the guest feels obligated to consider that you are taking his luggage down and loading it into his vehicle. This is not always true because when I take their luggage to the front of the hotel, I give the Doorman a few bucks to load his vehicle. You see, you can't violate the Doorman's property because the front of the hotel is his domain. You are not allowed to service anyone when he's on duty. However, all the Doormen loved me because on top of my tip, they will receive a tip from the guest. The Doorman capitalizes on that transaction.

So, I learned how to hustle on the job. Hustling came natural for me because growing up in a low-income environment where all of your peers competed to be better than you, made you strive harder than the next man. At a young age going to school without decent clothes on your back made you an outcast. Our neighborhood was very materialistic even though our parents were on welfare and making minimum wages on their jobs. However, this did not deter us from going into the streets to get what we needed to survive. So my mentality as a Bellman was to go after a dollar by any means necessary.

This brought to mind that I had to pick up a guest in room 1812 at 10 o'clock. I knew that this was Mrs. D and she had specifically requested me. I got goose bumps while going to her room because I didn't know what to expect. Upon my arrival, I noticed Gene (Bellman) at her door with a Bell Cart. I immediately made myself unnoticed and watched as he pulled away without any luggage on his cart. As he left, I proceeded to her room and knocked on the door. She opened the door with an enthusiastic smile and gave me a big hug while pulling me into the room.

"Shamar, I've been waiting for you. Who sent that other Bellman to my room? I requested you because I didn't want to check out without seeing you. Anyway, I sent him about his business," she said. Again, I was greeted by her in a provocative manner in that she was only wearing a slip that showed her luscious breasts. I couldn't help but wonder if she was trying to entrap me into a compromising position. I knew Gene had just left and could be lurking in the corridor to witness any indiscretion I may act upon. I began to get nervous and my thoughts were to hurry out the room.

"SET-UP", I thought! Maybe this wasn't the case, but I had to think about the meeting I had Mr. Gerritzen where Gene told him about me being in Mrs. D's room too long. The only thing I focused on was Gene trying to get even with me for getting out of that situation. My response to her was, "How are you today Mrs. D? Did you need me to get your vehicle out of the garage?" Her reply was yes and I grabbed her keys and left with her luggage immediately. I told her that I would be waiting in the lobby when she finished dressing. There wasn't time to waste; I felt I was being watched.

After I got her vehicle loaded, I gave the valet guy her keys and told him she would be down shortly. As I walked back into the lobby, Mrs. D was already checking out. I also noticed that Gene and Mr. Gerritzen were standing at the Bell Stand watching traffic in the hotel. Sometimes Managers take calls for us at the Bell Stand and direct us to which room needs help with their luggage. I was summoned to room 1753, which was Dr. Cook's room. As I grabbed a cart to leave, Mrs. D stopped me, handed me an envelope, and gave her farewell. It was a relief to see her leave. She was a beautiful person but her issues could also cost me my job.

As I entered the elevator to go to Dr. Cook's room, I opened the envelope. It was a two-page letter with a $100 bill enclosed. I nearly fainted and had to brace myself with the cart. I didn't have time to read the letter so I pocketed it until later. I proceeded to room 1753, loaded my luggage cart, and escorted Dr. Cook to the lobby. On the way down, he asked how I was getting along with Gene. Although I couldn't stand him, I didn't speak ill of another employee. In the hotel industry, you don't want the guests to feel they're in a negative atmosphere.

While waiting for my tip from Dr. Cook, one of the valet guys (Hussein) approached me in the Bell Closet. He started questioning me about going to the garage and getting a guest's vehicle (Mrs. D's). You see, every department in the hotel has certain duties that you are not allowed to cross (especially when there are tips to be made). The Valet department parked all vehicles because they are contracted by the hotel. The hotel is not responsible for any liability of guest vehicles. I definitely wasn't thinking when I did this because I could easily have been fired and there was nothing I could have said.

Hussein gave me a big scolding about doing his job and was very upset because Mrs. D did not tip at all. I realized that if he would have taken his complaint to one of the Managers – I would have been a goner. So, I had to think of a solution to curtail this drama. I said, "Listen, Hussein, what do I need to do to forget about this incident? I'm very sorry I overstepped my boundaries and please forgive me for disrespecting your job. Take this $10 and let's shake on it." Hussein gave me a big smile and said, "Okay Shamar. We're cool." He shook my hand and the case was closed. I was relieved and turned my attention back to Dr. Cook.

After Dr. Cook finished checking out, I proceeded to take his luggage outside to the Doorman. This was my first convention since being hired and it was very profitable. I regretted that this was the last day but was informed that things were not about to slow down. The next day there was another convention checking in. Mr. Gentry told me to rest well that night because the largest Black female Sorority 20,000 strong was invading our city. He said our hotel will be checking in about 500 of them. As I mentioned our hotel was connected to the Convention Center, which made it convenient for Conventioneers.

While finishing our day, all the Bellmen were gossiping about the thrill of the next day. Everyone was anticipating getting their pockets swelled with cash because these ladies had a reputation of being big tippers. Why not – they were all College Graduates who used their degrees to land corporate salaries. These women were mostly single, independent, and loaded, I was informed. One Bellman who had experienced the last Convention here told me that they love to party and are very direct on what their needs are. This excited me and I asked for details on that statement.

The only response he gave was to keep my mind open and go for the ride. I didn't know how to interpret that statement, but he left with a big simile. It happened that Precious was standing there and said, "Listen Shamar, I'll tell you what he meant. These KAK girls are wild and freaky. They're here to practice what they did in college and that's to fuck any fine man they can. So be careful because they're going to be all over you, Rick and Charles." I took her statement as sarcasm and realized that she was still angry with me from our last encounter.

This was what you call player hating. My only thought was that I had to reach out to the valet guys and win their respect. I realized that I had to bond with them because they could ruin any chances of me fulfilling a guest's needs. Say for instance, a guest asked me to retrieve something they left in their vehicle. I must be able to quickly carry out this task without any problems. Usually it's the Valet Service that does this – they have the guest's car-keys in their possession. Like I said, every department has their jobs defined and if I was going to make any money, I must be able to do whatever's requested of me.

Therefore, this gave me the incentive to call a private meeting with all the Valet guys. I had to keep in mind that all these guys were of foreign origin. Some were Africans, some were of Middle-Eastern descent, but I had to make sure my dialect was compassionate and non-authorative. I didn't want them to feel that I was taking over their jobs without reward.

One thing I knew about the Africans was that they were very domineering in their heritage, especially the Muslims. They do not accept anyone invading on their territory. After getting them all together I said, "Listen gentlemen, as you know my name is Shamar and I've just been here a few weeks. I want to say that I feel that you're all my brothers in Islam and if there's anything I can do for you, please don't hesitate to ask me. We're all here for one objective and that is to provide a living for our families. First, I'm going to do anything that a guest requests of me, and if I request your assistance to fulfill this request, I will reward you every time. We're all here to make money and I'm not selfish. If you help me, I'll help you. So let's work together because every day is not going to be a good day."

After I finished my speech, I felt confident that I got through to them. The first person that came over to shake my hand was Hussein. All the other guys acknowledged that they would work with me because I appeared to be a straight-up guy. We left the Bell-closet to continue our duties. It was nearing time for me to leave for the day and I was called over to the Concierge's Stand. When I arrived, who was there waiting to see me – the guest whom I had taken to room 1011, JOHN COOK...This was the guest who met me at Club Elite and bought me a few shots.

As I approached, John had a desiring smile on his face as though I was a walking dessert. I got this feeling because of his demeanor when we met at Club Elite. He was very overt with his sexual preference while asking me about my personal life. I tried my best to stay composed but I did not have any patience with homosexuals. He said, "Hi Shamar, how are you today? I know you're about to get off work and I was wondering if you would stop and have a drink with me – I'm buying. I don't want you to think that I'm trying to hit on you, but I love your personality."

My first thought was that John Cook was full of shit! I've been around a long time and I know when a gay sees something they like, their goal is to consummate. I respect all sexual preferences a person has. I just know that I'm monogamous only with a female. My reply to him was, "Mr. Cook, thank you for the offer, but my fiancé is picking me up and we are going to dinner tonight. I enjoyed hanging out with you the other night, but I'm not really a bar person. I rarely go anywhere without the company of my fiancé. By the way, when do you check out?" He gave me a look of disappointment and said, "I haven't decided yet."

Well that was the end of our conversation. I knew my response to his offer would turn him off. Gay guys despise the thought of a woman having someone like me. I hoped this would end his flirtatious thoughts of me. Anyway, I got a call to pick up my last guest for the day. It was time for me to get off and I was ready. My pockets were full of money, I had a good rapport with the valet guys, and I ended what could have been a bad judgment of having the drink with Mr. Cook. My only thought was of the great day that lies ahead.

Now it was a coincidence that John Cook and Dr. Cook had the same last name – don't get it twisted, I know my characters. After I got my last guest checked out, I rushed to the time clock and headed to the locker room. Exhausting was an understatement to what I was feeling. I sat at my locker and took a deep breath. I nodded off for a moment and was awakened by Rick, (the other Bellman). "Wake-up Shamar!!! Boy, you must have had a great day. You got money on the floor." I didn't realize I was counting my tips while changing into my street clothes. Anyway, I was glad it was Rick that awakened me.

While on my way home, I could not help but reminisce of the day's events. I felt very proud of myself. I had handled every situation in a diplomatic nature. I kept a professional attitude that reflected on the hotel. Complements were given to me by every guest I serviced. Yes, my self-esteem had gone above the bar. My only thought was to get home, take a good long shower, have dinner and get a good night's rest because the next day was going to be busy. A big check-in laid ahead – KAK sorority – I couldn't wait. As I lay in bed, I pulled out the letter Ms. D had given to me and began to read it.

"Dear Shamar, thanks for the service you provided me at your hotel. Your managers are very lucky to have a dedicated employee like you. I'm following up with an email to your corporate office, letting them know how much of an asset you are to their company. If every employee there had your skills, they wouldn't need any managers. I'm really delighted how you made my stay there very pleasurable. Your significant other better watch out because I will steal you from her. You made me realize how much I miss having a gentleman in my life. Although I was trying to come on to you, you kept your dignity.

Listen Shamar, I work for a company whose home office is in your city. I'm at your hotel at least three times a year. I just want to know if I can get a refill when I return. I hope the tip I left you let you know I'm not a scrub (smile). If you save that hundred-dollar bill I left you, I'll give you another one when I return next month. Don't try to trick me because I put my mark on it. Good Luck. Ms. D (aka spoiled)."

New Agenda

I woke the next day with a new attitude. Every day in the hotel industry is exciting because you are challenged with a variety of complex personalities. Some guests leave home feeling relieved of the stress they endure with spouses, kids and work. These are the guests you love to service because they are receptive to everyone who's kind and offering their service for anything they desire. Now we know there is a limitation, but you must work inside their mind that they are special and you're there to make their stay as pleasurable as possible. This relieves any transgressions they have.

You must also be attentive to the guests who look at you as a servant of the hotel. These people are not considerate of anything you do and are not good tippers (if at all). They also are demanding on their needs and usually not cordial. When you encounter a guest with this demeanor, you try to avoid them or count it as a loss. I try to shower them with kindness while engaging conversation to break their spirit. Some people are withdrawn and don't communicate well, so you must try to break the ice by speaking of something they can identify with.

After getting my thoughts together, I was energized to confront the next big check-in. I was whisked away by Mr. Gentry when I clocked in for the day. He led me to his office and asked would I mind working the second shift. I didn't hesitate to accept this offer because that was the money shift. I would come in at 2:30pm for guest check in and get off at 10:30 in the evening. Check-in time for a guest was at noon and when I arrived the lobby was flourishing. Besides, I had more time to rest before reporting to work.

The only apprehension I had was that I would be working with Gene. I had to erase all negative thoughts I had about him in order for us to work together. You must be able to get along with your coworkers because there's a lot communication between you all. The money you make relies on the teamwork you all perform. I might have to assist you with luggage, watch your cart for you, answer the phone while you're gone, send special requests someone may ask, you name it – it's teamwork involved and you have to be honest with one another.

Well it was check-in day for the KAK Convention and we started getting busy. All the Bellmen were on duty and it looked as though we were going to have a prosperous day. Everyone was neatly dressed waiting their turn at the Bell Stand to take a guest to their room. The Doormen had Valet guys pulling carts of luggage into the lobby. The lobby was full of carts because these ladies brought an excessive amount of clothing. I was warned of this before their arrival, because they love to show each other how successful they've been.

It was unbelievable to see that one guest would have two carts full of luggage. This was pleasing for me because the more work you do – the more tips you would receive. These ladies were very appetizing to the eye and appeared to have lots of money. They dressed in designer clothes with matching accessories. The jewelry they wore was not Zircons but real diamonds. It was a show of whose who on the red carpet that day. I was just excited anticipating the money I was going to make from all of them.

I was posted at the hotel's entrance when I saw a young lady pulling her own luggage in. I immediately rushed over to her and offered my service, "Good morning, Welcome to The Grandeur Hotel. My name is Shamar and I'll be delighted to assist you, Miss." I grabbed her cart and escorted her to the check-in line. She said, "Thank you. Sir. I'm Willa and I'm here for the Convention. After I check in, will you take my luggage up?" I assured her that I was at her service and would be watching her luggage until she finished. This was my first guest of the day and I felt good about the results.

After taking this guest to her room, I was rewarded with a $20 tip. This was very encouraging because the average tip is $5 and that's from a preferred guest. Even if I average five dollars for each guest, servicing 100 Guests will net $500. Not a bad day ahead, I thought. Everything was going very well. We were getting guests to their rooms in a fast-pace; faster than I've ever seen the other Bellmen move. I guess everyone was hyped up on the kindness they were shown in their tips. Smiles were posted throughout the hotel.

As the day rushed on, I kept noticing Charles (Bellman) taking two or three luggage carts up to rooms. It was something strange about this because he never had any guests following him upstairs. Normally you wait until a guest checks in and then you escort them to their room. It was not unusual for a guest to have two carts, but at least you wait for them so you can get your tip after the delivery. Therefore, I thought I would relax behind the Concierge Stand and watch the moves Charles was making. After about 20-minutes my suspicion came to light. I was surprised at what I had witnessed.

Charles is playing the "Bump Game". When his turn came up to service a guest, he would grab another guest who was waiting and write their room number down and tell them that he would meet them in their room. This way you see him walking beside one guest, but he has already sent the other guest ahead. He may have three guest's luggage and that enables him to get tipped by three people on one trip. However, this was foul play because you can't bump another Bellman out of his tip. My feelings for Charles changed instantly and his greed made me despise him.

It was very difficult for me to continue working that day after seeing Charles use deceit on his fellow Bellman. This was a low blow that was as bad as stealing money out of our pockets. I didn't know how to handle the situation. I didn't know if I should tell the Manager or what. I did know that I was mad as hell and had to settle down before I approached Charles. As the day progressed, I realized it wouldn't be fair if the other Bellmen were not aware of his dishonesty. A thief is not to be trusted, especially if he stealing from you.

Anyway, business was at its peak and I could not take the time to address this episode. My greatest concern was to stop Charles immediately because he was taking money from my pocket. So I decided to approach him on the matter. As he passed me with a cart of luggage I said, "Listen man, I've been watching you and don't appreciate your moves. If you bump another Bellman, I'm going to blow your cover. I had more respect for you than that. Now don't let me catch you doing this again or we're going to have a problem. You should be ashamed of yourself for doing your co-workers this way."

Now I was talking to Charles as he was pulling his cart to a room. He never missed a step, nor did he look at me while I was talking to him. His attitude was not forgiving and he was unconcerned about the situation. I was taken-back by his attitude and got very frustrated. This gave me more grounds to bring this to the Manager's attention. I didn't want to be a snitch because this could have caused him to lose his job. But if he wasn't going to acknowledge me, he left me no choice. My alternative was to let the other Bellmen know and we could all sit down to discuss this with Charles.

So my decision was the latter, I thought I'll call all the Bellmen together for a meeting without the presence of any Managers. I thought that if we could resolve this matter – nobody would get hurt. This was a bold undertaking on my part because I didn't have any clout with the other Bellmen. I remind you that I was new on the job and I hadn't paved my leadership role in the group. If anyone took this role, it should be Precious because she was the most senior employee. However, I could not ignore the fact that this involved all of us without me taking a stance, it would be neglect on our welfare.

As the day went on, I was delighted with the tips I was receiving and to the end of the parade of beautiful women that were coming. I noticed that most of the guests were middle-aged women who were born doing the baby boom era. This made my appetite more delightful because they were my age. You see if you were born after World War II, it was a chance that you had a structured upbringing. Parents then had a chance to have the American dream and that was to get a job, get married, and raise your family in a productive life environment. This was the objective of our parents then.

After reminiscing on my upbringing, I had to come back to the current time and that was that I must now make a way of life for my family. As I was standing and almost in a daze, one guest approached me and said, "Sir, Sir, Sir, can you help me? I need some help with my luggage. There's nobody outside to help me unload my car." I turned around and it was a KAK guest needing help. For a moment, I was transfixed on her beauty but dollar signs took that place. "Yes, Miss. My name is Shamar and I'll be delighted to assist you," I said.

I went outside to retrieve her luggage but the Valet guy was already in motion. After loading the cart, I took hold and led the guest to her room. Along the way, I passed Charles and he gave me a long, unfriendly stare. I ignored him and continued my task. After leaving the guest's room, I came to the lobby and Charles was standing there to meet me. He signaled for me to join him in the Bell Closet. His first words were that he was sorry he offended me. The explanation for his actions wasn't sympathetic to me.

He said, "Listen man, don't blame my heart for cheating you guys out of your tips. I want to fess-up to you, man. I have a drug problem that's been kicking my ass and I don't have any control over it. This is why my greed takes over. Shamar, I need help, man. My life is falling apart as we speak. Before I came to work, my wife was packing her clothes to move in with her mother. My rent is two months past due and before today's over, I'll be looking for somewhere to stay. So please man, don't bring this to the attention of the other guys. I won't bump anyone else – I promise. I can't afford to lose my job, man."

Before I could respond to Charles' plea, Rick burst into the door to let me know it was my turn to take a guest to their room. I was surprised to see Precious, Gene and Martin all standing by the door listening to the conversation between me and Charles as I left the room. "What the fuck is happening with Charles ? I heard him pleading with you not to tell us what's going on. Is he up to his old tricks? I know he gets greedy when we have a big check-in. Now tell me what that bastard did now. Because if he is bumping again, I'm telling Management on his ass," said Precious.

It appears that I was the only one unaware of his tactics, so I told everyone I'll give them the scoop when I return off my Front. Oh! A Front is when it's your turn to take a guest to their room. It was too busy to get involved in a debate now, so I just regrouped and focused on making my money. The guest I was taking up even noticed the commotion we had going. "Bellman, you appear to be stressed out. Are you feeling ok?" she said. I introduced myself, welcomed her to our hotel then proceeded to her room.

The guest told me her name was Trina Jones and she was here for the KAK convention. She went on telling me how much she liked our city, hotel and was looking forward to letting her hair down. It was her first trip from home (New Mexico) in 10 years. This lady was very talkative and I listened attentively to her conversation. This was the first time I had ever met a black young woman from New Mexico in my life, so I had to hear her story. She went on to explain that after she graduated from college, her first job was there and she hadn't left.

It appeared to me that a breath of life had been pumped into her. This was Trina's first KAK Convention and she was ready to explore all the excitement that came with it. She asked me if I could suggest an adventure that she could take on. I paused for a moment and said, "How about a threesome? " She immediately came back and said," Oh Shamar that will be good, I haven't done that since my college days." This response shocked the shit out of me. I was only being sarcastic and was trying to stop her from running her mouth but I only opened a can of worms.

After unloading her luggage, she tipped me $20 and said she wanted to get back with me later that evening. I said "okay" and left her room. I must say that it was only midday and I found myself at the check-in desk exchanging small denominations for $20 and $50. This is a task that I usually saved until I got ready to checkout for the day, but guests were constantly flowing and being very generous. It was going so good that I had forgotten about the mishap with Charles, but the other Bellmen had not forgotten. They were waiting for my meeting with them.

I became frustrated with this dilemma and decided to end it. Besides, my attention was on servicing the guests – not worrying about petty theft. So I called all the Bellmen into the Bell Closet and said, "Listen everybody, you all know that Charles has a drug problem. You've known he has a habit. Now I caught him stealing carts from us and he swore he wasn't going to do it anymore. Let's keep an eye on him and if he does it again, let's just tell Management and get him out of our hair. I'm sure if security runs the tape, he will be exposed. Meanwhile, let's keep making tips."

Everyone dropped their heads and we decided to agree on another chance for Charles. As we left the Bell Closet everyone continued doing what we do best and that was getting guests in and out of the hotel with promptness. Even Mr. Gentry saw all of us coming to the lobby at once and was bewildered at what was going on. "Shamar, Gene, what's going on? All of you guys disappeared and now you're back. What's the problem?" Rick pulled Mr. Gentry to the side and whispered something in his ear. I saw Mr. Gentry laugh and that was the end of that.

I have no idea what he said but everything was cool. One thing I've learned in the hotel industry is that around every corner you may encounter a different scenario. It's like a movie being played out before your eyes. A Bellman has a unique job. His actions go beyond customer service. He must console, sympathize, be compassionate, and cordial. The greatest challenge is being able to read your guest's personality. This is the make or break point about the job. If you can ensure that a guest's needs are being taken care of before being asked, you are almost guaranteed a handsome reward.

While standing at the Bell Stand, a guest came over and inquired about her lost luggage at the airport. She just wanted to know had it arrived yet. So I went back to check for her. After not seeing her luggage, I returned to the Bell Stand and another guest was waiting also to check on her missing luggage. I had to disappoint them both because we had not received anything. I took both their names and room numbers and assured them that when their luggage arrived I would contact them. "Sir please take my cell number in case I'm not in my room because I need my clothes immediately", said the guest.

After taking her cell number, Precious said, "You see Shamar, that's what I was talking about. Those same two ladies just came and asked me to check on their luggage ten minutes ago. When they saw you appear, they came right back with the same shit. Them whores trying to get some dick. I told you that you guys are going to be targets for these guests." I thought that if anyone was dick hungry it was Precious. This is the same woman who tried to rape me in a guest's room. I put aside everything she said.

Whatever Precious said to me about those KAK Sisters, went in one ear and out the other. She was just a jealous and lonely woman, who came across as dominating without anyone to dominate. I noticed that when her front came up she didn't put on a welcoming persona as she did with other guests – especially men. This was an attitude that I must play down because I didn't have any negative feelings about guests. Suddenly, I noticed an Airport Luggage Handler approaching the Front Desk with a trail of luggage. I knew right away that this was the lost luggage the guests were inquiring about.

I immediately summoned him over to me and verified the names to determine if they were registered at our hotel. After confirmation, I started calling their rooms to give them notice that their bags had arrived. I knew that this would be an extra tip in delivering their luggage to their rooms. I had noticed that most of the Bellmen would just let them know that their luggage was here at the Bell Stand and they could come to pick it up. Even if the guest was not in their rooms when called, I would take their luggage to their rooms and leave a note on the desk letting them know that it was "Shamar" who delivered.

This tactic makes the guests feel important and relieved that their luggage wasn't lost for good. On top of a joyous feeling, they are usually in a mood to reward whoever was responsible for getting their luggage to them. I couldn't miss that recognition, so I would leave them a nice sympathetic note, – "Sorry for the inconvenience you have experienced - it is with great concern that I made sure your stay here is without any discomfort, your Bellman "SHAMAR". Sometimes you never hear anything back from a guest, but when you're not expecting, someone will come down and ask for you.

This made me remember to call the guest's cell phone when her luggage had arrived. She had stressed sternly that was what she wanted. So I called, "Hello, this is Patty. Can I help you?" I responded, "Yes, Miss, My name is Shamar and I'm the Bellman at the hotel. I just wanted to inform you that your luggage has arrived from the airport and I have it in my possession." She was very excited and thanked me for my concern. She said she was on her way back to the hotel and would stop at the Bell Stand on her way in. I assured her that I would safely watch over her luggage and to call when she arrived.

After talking to Patty, I was rushed off to take other guests to their rooms. My most important guest of the day was to escort the Chairman (CEO) of the KAK Convention to her suite. Her name was Mrs. Charlene Daniels and she was trailed by GM (General Manager, Mr. Sutter), and our managers, Mr. Gentry and Mr. Gerritzen. Usually when a CEO of a convention checks in, the managers make special accommodations to make sure all her requests are being met. You have to realize that she is responsible for bringing thousands of dollars to the hotel. Their objective is to suck up to her and make sure she's satisfied with the service.

Mr. Sutter brought Mrs. Daniels over to me and introduced me as the Bellman who would be taking her to her suite. "Mrs. Daniels, this is Shamar, one of our best Bellman in the hotel. Whatever you need, please let him know and he will accommodate you. Please let me know if there is anything that he can't handle and I will personally be of service." She acknowledged his gratitude and we left the lobby for her suite. She had two carts of luggage that was very heavy and caused me problems with maneuvering. Charles came to my rescue and said, "Shamar, I'll take one up with you and you don't owe me a thing."

I was somewhat surprised to see his concern in this matter because I was having difficulty moving her luggage. It was a common understanding that when you assist another Bellman with their front, you're entitled to a split on the tip. Charles assured me that this was a freebie on him. His politeness made me only think that he was saying thanks for saving him from the remorseful situation that occurred earlier that day. After arriving at Mrs. Daniels' suite, Charles disappeared like Houdini (the magician). He left me with a somewhat remorseful feeling because I had come at him in a threatening mode.

Anyway, my attention remained on the business at hand, and that was to get Mrs. Daniels settled in her suite. I figured that since she was the lady in charge of this convention, she would be honored to have great service. After unloading all her luggage, I offered to unpack for her. She refused the offer but was very appreciative for the thought. She said, "You are such a polite Bellman but you probably don't want to see what I have in my bags." However, she did have one request for me and that was to make sure that I bring her roommate up when she arrived.

"Listen Shamar, I really like your service. The guest's name is Janet Richards and she will be checking-in shortly. Make it your business that you are the Bellman who delivers her to my room – OK", she said. I assured her that I would be on watch for her and would bring her up. Mrs. Daniels handsomely tipped me and I departed for the lobby. Twenty-five dollars was a delightful tip for one guest. If my day continues like that, I'll leave here smiling.

Party Time

I wondered why the hotel was named "The Grandeur", so I went to the dictionary to find its meaning. Grandeur (a) the quality of being impressive or awesome. This was a perfect title because it described what we are for our guests. With that thought in mind, I continued my day with an upbeat attitude. Suddenly, I was interrupted from going to lunch by Mr. Gentry. He said there was a guest who just checked in and only requested my service. Little did I know that it was Ms. Richards. Mrs. Daniels had already called her in advance to request me as her Bellman.

I noticed that the other Bellmen were standing in line waiting for their front, but I was chosen before them. This created some animosity because they were jealous because I was preferred over them. As I passed them, I gave off a proud blush, but I felt the knives in my back as I approached Ms. Richards. But I didn't let it deter me from possibly receiving another twenty-five dollar tip. "Good afternoon Ms. Richards. My name is Shamar and I've been expecting you. Welcome to The Grandeur Hotel. I am here to make your stay as pleasurable as possible. Just follow me and I'll take you up to your suite."

She gave off a delightful smile, so I grabbed her cart and proceeded to her suite. As we arrived, Mrs. Daniels was already at the door to greet us. It's been four years since they have seen each other and they were very elated. I continued to unload her luggage and asked if there was anything else I could do for them. She said, "Shamar, there is one thing I would like to request of you. I'm having a meet-and-greet reception this evening in my suite and if you can recommend someone to serve cocktails for us, I would surely appreciate it."

As she was handing me a twenty-dollar tip, I assured her that I would find someone and would give her a call back. She said that all her girls should be checked in by 5:00 PM and she needed that service by 6:00 PM. I thanked her and left the suite wondering who I could find for her. I would have loved to be the one, but I'll still be on duty. As I entered the lobby, I saw Phil (Doorman) leaving work for the day. Phil was a gentleman around 60 years old and he was very diplomatic. He was charming and very personable and I thought he would be a great candidate for the job as a Server.

"Phil, wait a moment. I'd like to speak with you", I said. I explained the job and duties to him and he immediately asked how long the job was and how much it paid. I told him it was for four hours at $10 an hour plus tips. He agreed without hesitation. I told him to be back at the hotel by 5:00 PM and bring a waiter's jacket. We shook hands on the deal and he went home in good spirits. I felt relieved because I knew he was someone who Mrs. Daniels and Ms. Richards would be comfortable with. They were about the same age and he was a handsome gentleman.

Before I parted for lunch, I gave Mrs. Daniels a call to inform her that my mission was accomplished and it would be a gentleman by the name of Phil who would be reporting to her.

She responded, "Thank you Shamar, I knew I could count on you. You have that gifted personality that would make anyone believe in you. I wish you were going to volunteer your service because you would have been a delight for the girls. But don't worry I'm going to take good care of you for doing this for me. The Manager told me to ask you for anything I needed and you would come through!"

As I finished my lunch, I returned to the lobby. There was a stream of guests still waiting to check-in for the KAK Convention. Bellmen were doing overtime because we couldn't keep up with the pace. Managers were taking guests to their rooms and this was not a norm. Although exhaustion was getting the best of us, we stayed focused on getting everyone to their rooms. Things subsided later in the day, which brought about great rewards for everyone. It was normal to see a Bellman counting hundreds of dollars in tips. Even Charles was making enough where he didn't have to bump anyone.

It was a great two days to see yourself making at least five hundred dollars. Never would I have thought that this kind of money could be made in a hotel. Our salary was below minimum wage, but who cared. It didn't make any difference because you were taxed for whatever you said you made in tips. As I stood at the Bell Stand, a worker from Guest Services informed me that a guest was ready to check-out of room 1011. It took me one minute to figure out that it was John Cook (gay guy). I looked around to see if there was another Bellman available, but there was not.

I purposely ignored the request because I didn't want to see him again. I was still offended by him making sexual overtures at me, so I continued to service other guests. I saw Gene exiting the elevator and I said, "Gene, I got a hot one for you. Go to room 1011. A guest is waiting to check-out." He did an about-face and caught the same elevator that had brought him down. "Thanks Shamar, I'm on my way," he said. I just laughed at him and continued on my tasks since I was told to get John Cook, it didn't matter because a service is fulfilled.

It was now 5:00 PM and Phil was just walking into the hotel. I was thrilled to see him because this guaranteed my payment for hiring him. I called up to Mrs. Daniels' suite to inform her that her server was here and on his way up to her suite. She assured me that she was grateful and would take care of me later. I pulled Phil aside and gave him a briefing on what his duties were. After our conversation, he proceeded up to Mrs. Daniels' suite. I was really fired up after this. My only desire now was to get off work and to the Club Elite for a nice drink.

The day was very profitable and it was coming to an end. While I was at the Guest Check-in Desk cashing in my small bills, someone tapped me on the shoulder. As I looked around it was John Cook informing me that he was checking out of the hotel. He expressed his pleasure to have met me. I gave him the same compliment and we parted ways. However, Gene wasn't too happy because Mr. Cook did not tip him for his service. He said, "Shamar did that guy give you a tip for me? I saw him talking to you. What's up?" I explained to Gene that he was only saying good-bye and didn't give me a dime. A frustrated look came over Gene's face.

My only concern now was to finish exchanging my money and get the hell off work. The only pleasure I thought about was going home, taking a shower and calling a Sweetie over to pleasure me before I went to sleep. It was comforting to know that I had satisfied every guest who I serviced that day. From delivering a guest's lost luggage to providing Mrs. Daniels a server for her event, it was a proud accomplishment for me. So as I left the hotel that evening, I was too tired to stop at Club Elite for a drink. Homeward bound was my only thought.

As I arrived home that evening, my significant other was parked in front of my house. I had called her as soon as I hit the time clock. She didn't waste any time getting to me because I told her that my testosterone level was at its peak. It had been a stressful day at work and I needed some sexual healing to relax me. When I approached her vehicle, she arose wearing a black trench coat. She opened the coat and said, "Are you ready for this baby?" There she stood in the street, wearing nothing but a garter strap and hose.

I immediately got a chubby and hurried her inside my house. I had been seeing beautiful women all day at work and my imagination was overflowing with sex. After taking a hot shower, I got into bed and succumbed to the affection my girl was giving me. After an hour of love-making, we paused so that I could count my tips for that day. After separating the mixed bills, we came to a total of six hundred seventy-six dollars. This was an amazing total. It made me realize that I averaged eighty-four dollars an hour. This was a good day and I thanked the Lord.

The next day at the hotel was another busy one. This was the first day for the KAK meetings and workshops. When there's a big Convention like this, you always have the late arrivals who rush you to their rooms so they can register and make all the events. I was just thrilled to see them pour in, regardless of what they requested. I had made up in my mind that whatever the request was, I would fulfill it. Speaking of fulfillment, the guest who I spoke with on the previous day (Patty) approached me and took me up on that threesome that she hadn't experienced since her wild days in college. "Hello Shamar, do you remember me? You told me that you could make it possible for me to let my hair down. Can you make my request possible? I would love for you to be a participant, "she said.

I wasn't ready for anyone to be so bold, so for a moment, I was speechless. I told her that I would get back to her that night. She gave me a big hug and said not to let her down. She went on to express that life was passing her by and the reason she came to the Convention was to explore new adventures. At this point, I didn't want to include anyone on this caper.

Life in the whole industry proved to be more exciting than I imagined. I didn't realize that you could make money and get your freak on at the same time. I was in heaven, but I never forgot to thank God for giving me the blessing of another chance in life. Remember, you're not a spring chicken. After fifty years of age, you've got to count all your eggs. I looked back on my childhood and realized that I was taking life for granted. Most of my peers were dead or in jail, but I'm still surviving and in decent health.

After giving Patty confirmation, I proceeded with my duties. While standing at the front door of the hotel talking to

Phil about last night's events, Mrs. Daniels came up. "Oh Shamar, I've been looking for you. Oh, hi Phil. Everything went well last night and I really appreciate it. Here's a little something I promised you." I extended my hand and she handed me a fifty dollar bill! " Thank you Mrs. Daniels and if there's anything else I can do for you, please call me." After she walked away, Phil also thanked me because he made one hundred dollars that evening. Again, a typical satisfying day was accomplished at The Grandeur.

Although I was unable to work Mrs. Daniels' event, there would be more opportunities ahead. The KAK Sorority was known for their hard partying. While at the Bell Stand, I noticed Willa Johnson (Room 822) approaching. She's a KAK member who I checked into the hotel. Her physique would make any woman jealous. "You know what I need Shamar? I need four male strippers at my party tonight. I got twenty women who are very horny and need some attention," she said. My response was, "Why do you need so many, I could accommodate you with two male strippers and you'll be satisfied."

I knew that having too many dancers would stretch the money too far. My greatest challenge was where was I going to find two male strippers. That's why I say that a good Bellman's job is obligational. Guests request things of you that are outside the policies of the hotel. If the General Manager knew I was soliciting whores or strippers in his hotel that would be the end of my job. My only service to the guests is to escort them and their luggage to the rooms. Personal relationships are not allowed. But the only way you can make some money is to deviate.

I knew Willa's request was going to cost me a few dollars but I couldn't make myself ask her to provide the money up front. You see, when you give a fee for your service that's all you can expect. But when you provide the service yourself, the guest is obligated to ask you then what was their bill. It's like when you check out of the hotel, the clerk tabulates all your charges, phone calls, room service, etc., and gives you a total of your charges. Although my services aren't contractual, you must be able to evaluate which guests have money to pay you back. So, you are gambling – you may win or you may lose.

However, I felt good about this request because these ladies were not broke. I knew that if I could pull this off, my status at being the go-to-guy would ensure that everyone would feel comfortable dealing with me. That was the whole objective to being a Bellman. You must win confidence in guests that indicates that you are personable and can make things happen for them. I had to think down the line when I returned to the hotel and the only person they can remember is Shamar. This would give me an advantage over the other Bellmen. My immediate thought now was how I was going to find two male exotic dancers....

First, I had to find out from Willa where she was going to have the party that night. She explained that after she conducted a workshop in one of our conference rooms, they were going to use Mrs. Daniels' suite for the party. This gave me more incentive because the word-of-mouth was working well for me. I assumed that after satisfying Mrs. Daniels with her meet-and-greet party, she recommended me to Willa.

The only person I could think that would help me was "Stevie", the owner of Club Elite. He had a club in the Red Light District and was well connected to all the Strip Club owners, so I gave him a call. After explaining my scenario to him, he agreed to help me out. He said, "Listen Shamar, you're a good friend of mine and I respect you dearly. Don't worry about a thing. I'll have two guys at your hotel by 11:00 PM. That's a small request for me; give me something that's a challenge." I told him that I appreciated it very much and he relieved me of a lot of worry. I asked him how much it was going to cost me. "Don't worry brother – it's on me", he said, "Case closed."

After confirming everything between Stevie and Willa, I felt relieved. I had just accomplished something that was new to me. I knew I couldn't let anyone know of my endeavors here at the hotel... I was praying that none of the Sorority sisters let the cat out of the bag. Can you imagine if the other Bellmen knew that I was out-hustling them? Yes, that would be a problem for me. I washed the thought away and dwelled on how much I was going to charge Willa for my service. Although it hadn't been a dime out of my pocket, I had to give her an expense.

Whatever I charged her, it was going to be straight profit. So I went to the Bell Closet and pondered my figures. I had no idea what Stevie's agreement with them was, but I knew they mainly depend on tips. I concluded that I would say I gave them fifty dollars each to appear and hoped she would tip me for my efforts. Anyway the evening passed by very quickly and I found myself staying over waiting for the dancers' arrival. Finally, two gentlemen came through the door. We introduced ourselves and I asked had Stevie taken care of them. They assured me he did and I led them to their job.

After taking Willa her dancers, she asked how much it was going to cost her. I told her that she wasn't worrying about the cost when she asked me to get her some strippers, so whatever you think it's worth, I will accept it. She said, "OK Shamar, this is what I did. I knew my request was outside the norm and I didn't expect you to come through. However, I asked all the girls to contribute to the cost and we came up with two-hundred dollars. Will that be enough?" I was amazed with the number and I gratefully thanked her and wished her a great evening.

Well, that was the end of the day for me. I had been at the hotel for twelve hours and it was time to celebrate. I had thoughts of staying around until the party ended to see what was going to be available after the freak show. But I could not give myself away to jealous co-workers. So I stopped at my usual spot, Club Elite to thank Stevie for his generosity. He was totally responsible for me making two-hundred dollars with no effort. I owed him a great deal of gratitude and was determined to cut him in on a piece of my profit.

When I arrived at Club Elite, the first person I saw was Precious looking fabulous. As I mentioned, she was a very beautiful woman who dressed well. Her wardrobe was on the same style as Phyllis Hyman, the legendary songstress. Our eyes were affixed on each other as I walked into the club. She had been off work for several hours and appeared that she had gotten her drink on. As I approached the bar to order, she said, "Hi Shamar, I see you are keeping late hours at work. I assume your pockets are fat, from the extraordinary work you put in today."

Usually when Precious makes a statement to me it's very sarcastic and this wasn't any different. Although she gave me an alluring smile, I knew she was aware of the services that I provided Willa and Mrs. Daniels. She just came out and said, "Listen Shamar, nothing happens in that hotel that gets past me. Willa asked me first about providing male strippers. I told her, you're the only person that could make that happen. I was looking out for you boy and wanted you to make that money.

Now if you want to show me your appreciation, let's get together tonight."

This attitude goes back to when I started working at the hotel. It was Precious who first welcomed me with gratitude of sex with her. I see things haven't changed and she's determined to get me. Now don't get me wrong, I'm sure I would enjoy the pleasure of being with her, but her dominance was a turn-off for me. However, I felt very good this evening and my temptation for her body overrode any sense of reasoning that came to mind. My response to her was, "Precious, thank you very much for that gesture. I'll be glad to strip for you tonight."

After my conversation with her, I had to turn my focus back to what I came there for and that was to talk with Stevie, the owner. I asked the Bartender if Stevie was available and she said he was in his office taking care of business. So I just joined Precious at her table and ordered us a bottle of Moët Champagne. She was deserving of anything she requested of me. After all, were it not for her, I wouldn't be the recipient of the two-hundred dollar tip I received earlier. I didn't' realize that she was that concerned with my welfare.

The atmosphere was vibrant as usual in the Club that night and I was having a pleasant encounter with Precious. We talked, danced and drank Moët all evening until closing. Our relationship had been bittersweet with no love for each other, but tonight was different. I guess what had me open was that finally I was going to get that coochie!!! She did not let me forget that I was going to her house tonight. Well, it was closing time at the club and Precious and I headed to her vehicle. "Who's driving? You or me", she said.

I took her keys and volunteered. The emphasis now was to make sure I wasn't too tipsy to drive. I knew she wasn't in any shape so I had to make do. After arriving at her house, she asked was I planning to spend the night. I told her we'll see how the night flows and decide from there. She agreed and we entered the house. Her house was very neat and tranquil. That made me relax without second thoughts about going home that night. She relaxed herself by changing into a sexy teddy. After an invite to the bedroom, lights were off.

I made it home the next morning with a hangover. Precious had dropped me off early because she had to be to work at 6:00 AM. We all sometimes have regrets for something we've already done. Do you ever wish that it would go away? Well, that's not possible and you wind up living life with a little guilt. That's the way I felt after realizing what I had done with Precious. We made love all night and that wasn't my intention. I had violated my oath to never have a sexual affair with anyone I work with. But, I had allowed lust to overrule.

Anyway, it was another day and I still had time to rest before going to work at 2:00 PM. So, I relaxed in my bed and counted yesterday's receipts that totaled five-hundred dollars –

another good day at The Grandeur Hotel. I went to work with another positive attitude. My spirits were high and I let go all the regrets I had for the previous day. I prepared myself with a prayer to God before I entered the hotel to begin work.

"LORD THANK YOU FOR THE BLESSINGS YOU GIVE ME EVERYDAY. I KNOW THAT I AM NOT PERFECT, SO PLEASE WATCH OVER ME."

Another day – another dollar....That was my phrase as I checked in to start my day. I always arrive thirty minutes early before I start. I love to sit in the employee's café and grab a bite to eat. This was my favorite time to catch everyone who's leaving for the day. This really is the highlight of my day because I usually get all the information of what occurred before my arrival. Employee gossip about their adventures and misfortunes with guests they encountered that day. This gives me a somewhat advantage on where and when to abstain from a guest's demands.

It's hard for me to explain, but the hotel industry is a city within itself. Everyone knows each other's business and I am sure Precious would let everyone know that I smashed her. Either I was going to get disrespected or become a desired person to have sex with. But that depends on the rumor Precious put out on me. She could tell everyone I was a dead fuck and did not pleasure her. Or she could tell the truth that I was the best fuck she ever had, at least that is what she told me. Whatever it is, I knew I was going to be the newest gossip of the hotel.

When I arrived in the lobby, the first person I saw was Willa. She had just left a luncheon in one of our banquet rooms. She gave me accolades on the fine service I had provided to her the previous night. She said, "Shamar, the girls really enjoyed the dancers last night and some got a little extra after it was over. I really appreciate your service. Do you provide any other service for individuals?" I didn't know how to evaluate that question because it was left open. I decided to ignore her because it was time for me to chill.

After talking to Willa, I saw Precious, Rick, Gene and Charles standing at the Bell Stand giving me a jealous stare. As I approached, Precious gave me a hug and kiss on the jaw. I was embarrassed by her action because everyone knew we didn't get along well. I didn't know if she was being smart or really being affectionate. The only thing I could do was reminisce about our enjoyment we had making love the previous night. I just spoke to everyone and proceeded on.

Keeping It Moving

This was business week for the KAK Sorority. They flooded the Lobby, Restaurants and Concierge Desks asking for directions. There was traffic throughout the whole downtown area with members moving about their business. The first shift of Bellmen was getting off work, which only left Gene and me on duty. As Precious was leaving, she came over and asked me to give her a call when I got off. I immediately pulled her to the side and explained to her that we were not going to form a relationship. I told her that we both had a moment last night and let's forget about it.

She had a frown on her face and stormed out the hotel. At the same moment Mr. Gentry approached me and asked why did Precious have an attitude. I told him that I had no idea and I left his company. Business was going on as usual in the hotel and guests were constantly streaming in and out. My attention was called to a guest who needed someone to come to his room and pick up some packages to be taken down to the FedEx store for shipment. It was my Front and I exited the lobby to go to his room.

The guest who had called was an old veteran of the hotel. He also was a Premier Guest who was the CEO of a nationwide prestigious law firm. One of his firms was located in our city and he visited at least twice a year. He was very important to the hotel because he recommended a lot of business. When he checks in there's usually about ten people in his party. It's not unusual for him to have the most expensive conference room reserved for a week. I guess this is where he meets with all his attorneys to discuss future business and cases they're involved in.

His name was Charleston Everet. He maintained a suite on the top floor of the hotel. As I proceeded to his suite, I could not help but think what kind of tip I was going to receive for his service. Keep in mind that I worked in a five-star hotel and the guests that checked in were not tight with their wallets. If you're paying four hundred dollars a night, it's only customary that you take care of anyone who provides you service. That means from the Valet guys, Doormen and Bellmen.

After arriving at this suite, I greeted him, "Hello Mr. Everet, my name is Shamar and I'm here to pick up your packages." He invited me in and led me to the table where two large boxes were located. "Listen Shamar, I need you to take these down to the FedEx store. I already have them labeled. Just tell them to charge the cost to my master account." Without a response, I loaded the boxes on my cart and started to exit the room when he grabbed me and handed me a fifty-dollar bill. I thanked him politely and headed to the FedEx store.

I was truly blessed to have landed a job in such a prestigious hotel. My tenure has been very profitable as well as delightful. This was the only job I really looked forward to and enjoyed. The guests were generally polite as well as adventurous. Opportunities always arose where you can take advantage of someone's ignorance and kindness. Nevertheless, you had to keep in perspective that you were there to help people, not to use them. I learned that kindness was better than weakness and you would gain more. A fifty-dollar tip makes you aware of that.

After leaving the FedEx store, I encountered the guest who I had checked in room 842 (Trina Jones). I remembered that she was the KAK member who was looking forward to having a delightful experience while here in our city. She said, "Hello Shamar, how are you tonight? Listen, I was at the party that Willa sponsored and I heard that you had hooked that up. It was a job well done and I enjoyed the gentlemen entertainment. What would it cost me for the same two men for my pleasure?"

I lost my voice, before I could give a response. It was hard for me to believe that she would approach me with such a request. This was a young woman who was very desiring and with a high aptitude. She wouldn't have any problem finding someone that fit her standards. From my previous experience with her, I knew she was straightforward and was very liberal about sex. However, you're never prepared for a woman to approach you and ask you to hook her up with someone. Anyway, my response was that I had no way of contacting the gentlemen.

I knew I had to be smart and not get myself into any more episodes that would broadcast my name. If she had heard that I sponsored the freak show that Willa had, I would be vulnerable for any transgressions that come along. Although she wasn't happy with my reply, she came back with an alternative proposal. "Shamar, I know how that can be. You probably didn't really know those guys, but you were doing Willa a favor. I'm sorry if I offended you. Please forgive me," she said. I told her that it was no harm done and she continued along her way.

While standing at the Bell Stand, I noticed Mr. Gentry taking the police and security officers into his office. This was very unusual that we have police at the hotel. Something was going on. However, I continued taking guests to their room and doing my daily duties as a Bellman. It wasn't long when one of the Valet guys motioned me to the Valet room. This was a room where all Valet persons stored the keys for the guests who drive their own vehicles to the hotel. This was also the place where they would hang out and shoot the shit when not busy. The valet guy's name was Hakeem and he wanted to tell me what was going on with the police.

I asked him what was going on and he said, "You know we had an imposter come in front of the hotel and pose as a Valet guy. When the guest drove up, the imposter took the vehicle as though he was going to park it. We have not seen him or the vehicle since. Phil (Doorman) said that he saw everything but thought he was one of us. That's why the police are here making a report. Boy! That guest is pissed off." The answer to my curiosity had just been solved. It wasn't very long after the police left that Mr. Gentry summoned Gene and me to his office.

He had already gathered the Valet staff and we were cramped in his office. He began by stating what had happened to our guest's vehicle, which I already knew. His greatest concern was that no other Valet staff was out front with this imposter. He sternly stressed that he wanted at least two Valet guys out front at all times, regardless of the weather condition. He shouted, "There was no excuse why this happened and if I walk outside and don't see a Valet guy on duty, I'm going to fire the Supervisor on down. Meeting over!!!"

It was getting late in the evening and Hotel Security was patrolling more than usual. I was told by Tim (Security Officer) that they had captured the whole incident on the camera outside. They had a clear picture of the car thief on film. However, nobody had ever seen this guy. It was hard to believe that he came up randomly without notice and swiped a car. I personally felt that it was an inside job. Anyway, that was a myth that didn't have any substance. I had observed the Valet operation when I first applied but wasn't impressed with the tips they received.

Although the Valet staff aren't employees of the hotel, they are a great asset. Imagine checking into a five-star hotel and you had to park your own vehicle. That would be disappointing. You see after unloading your heavy luggage, you then must drive one block to the six-story garage, which is humongous. Then you walk back to the hotel to check-in. God forbid if the weather is bad - rain, snow, hot, etc. So the Valet service is great, but guests do not compensate them for their work. I rarely see a guest give a tip when they hand them their keys.

Being a Bellman is only one job you have in the hotel industry, but it transcends into many responsibilities. You have to wear many hats because guests feel that you are obligated to serve them. You may have a guest approach you to retrieve their vehicle out of the garage. Although they self-parked their vehicle, they do not want to take the long walk back to the garage. Sometimes you have a guest who will unload their own luggage into the garage and roll it back to the hotel. Whatever the scenario is you're usually asked to play a role. It's no different with the Valet guys, they get special requests also.

Since I had established a relationship with the Valet guys, I didn't feel obligated to pick up guest's vehicles or go to the garage with them to retrieve their luggage. This gesture usually warranted a handsome tip. Not only was it time-consuming, but you're dragging a cart of luggage for a long distance while being careful not to get struck by other vehicles. Like I said, it is not always a pretty job, but the rewards are great. The disappointing thing about this service is when you have a guest who's not appreciative and doesn't give you anything.

Disappointment comes with the territory of being a Bellman. There are days when you're on duty all day and you don't receive any tips. Of course, slow check-in days and walk-ins are expected. But, it was surprising to me that you can measure what you earn in tips by the ethnic group that checks in. Members of some nationality groups don't believe in rewarding for service you provide them. I thought they were just being cheap but Gene explained to me that some countries and cultures have been proving this for years.

"Don't get mad, Shamar, when you don't get tipped by certain races. In their country they believe that if they patronize your business you are obligated to provide them with service," Gene said. Although I didn't understand, I had to accept what it was. I always felt regardless of what a person's creed was, my charming personality would win them over. Demonstrating these ethics has given me a positive attitude about every race. You can't judge a person by the color of their skin, but by the content of their character, as Martin Luther King Jr. said.

Anyway, today's drama was running its course with Gene and me. It's been quite a while since we had a dilemma, so I guess it was time. Gene is a very greedy Bellman who gets jealous if you're making more tips than him. He's always watching every move I make. Even if I go outside and stand out front with the Doorman, momentarily Gene will appear wondering what I'm doing. He had accused me of taking the guest's luggage up to the side door of the hotel by-passing the lobby so he couldn't see me.

It was his Front and about two hours went by without a check in or out. He got delirious when I disappeared for a while. When I did return, I got off the lobby elevator counting some cash. With the stress of my not being in his sight and not knowing where I was, it was perplexing to him. He knew that I was a dedicated Bellman who remained on post regardless of how slow it was. He approached me and said, "Where you been Shamar, taking a guest up to their room? You know it was my turn to take the next guest up." I looked at him and answered yes.

This response did not sit well with Gene. I noticed him getting red in the face as if I had struck him. This attitude reminded me of the time when I first started and Gene told the

Manager that I was in a guest's room for a long time. I got reprimanded for this accusation that could have caused me to lose my job. I knew Gene was very vindictive if insulted, so I used this assumption to see how far he would go. I didn't make the situation any better when I started counting my proceeds at the Bell Stand in front of Gene. I knew this was enraging him because he had had a terrible day.

My hope was that he got mad enough to go tell another story to the Manager about me taking his Front. Gene makes himself believe whatever he assumes you did. Other Bellmen have already told me about Gene's desire to be in control and knowing where and what others are doing. However, I've experienced people like Gene and it didn't bother me. I just learned to use reverse psychology on the individual who's trying to ruin my life. I never did want to submit to Gene's attitude, because he was too greedy and disrespectful.

I immediately diverted my attention from Gene as one of the KAK Sorority members approached me at the Bell Stand. It was Trina Jones (room 842), again. She wanted to know where the Hot Spots were where a woman could go to have a good time. Her request was accentuated with a little, but slow, lip wipe with her tongue as though desire was her passion. I gathered this by her revealing to me how freaky she could be and there were no boundaries in her sexual exploits. The only thing I thought was that she was a lonely woman who needed a man's attention.

Trina was a beautiful woman who appeared to be forty-five years of age. She didn't wear any make-up and her hair was natural with a low cut. Her body was proportional to her height of approximately 5'10", which is my height. I didn't pay much attention to her beauty until I realized my needs and desires. She approached me at the right time because I was in a bad moment with Gene and I needed some relief. I was praying that Trina wasn't approaching me again about hooking her up with some man. If so, I was going to offer myself to soothe her passion.

Sometimes women use stories as a diversion from what they really feel and desire. I may have been wrong, but I felt Trina was trying to get my attention and I was the guy she desired. I don't mean to be conceited but a man knows when a woman is trying to hit on him. She has approached me at least four times about hooking her up and I was in denial each time. Like I said, I didn't want my name mentioned anymore with any of our guests. My experience with Ms. D gave me good insight on how this could be detrimental to my career here at the hotel.

While I was talking to Trina, I noticed that Gene was inching his way closer to us so he could hear our conversation. From our last episode with Ms. D, I knew he was trying to find some incriminating evidence to report to Mr. Gentry or Mr.

Gerritzen. However, I did not give him the satisfaction of hearing our conversation, because I took Trina outside. The longer Trina and I talked, I found myself being attracted to her. Our conversation had gotten personal as we discussed what we both were looking for in life. We both concluded that we were looking for a significant other.

Before Trina and I departed company, she said, "Shamar, I hope I wasn't too open in disclosing how I feel about you. It is somewhat embarrassing for me because some men look at this as weakness in a woman. However, I'm just a grown woman who goes after what she wants. I don't know anything about you, but I certainly would love to find out, if you're willing." I responded by letting her know that I was definitely interested in getting to know more about her and continuing a relationship. "Listen Trina, I got to get back to work and when I get off, I'd love to take you to dinner," I said. She responded, yes.

As the evening progressed, I noticed that Gene wasn't being sociable at all with me. I would try to engage him in conversation but he would only respond with a one-liner. My patience with his ignorance always reminded me that I must be the better man and not let his attitude affect my performance in my job. Anyway, my thoughts were centered on my conversation with Trina and where I was going to take her to dinner that evening. Although it would be late when I got off, I knew of a restaurant that serves food until 1:00 AM.

Usually the hotel's traffic dies after 9:00 PM. Guests do not check in or out of the hotel this late. I found this a great opportunity to leave work two hours early. I knew before I would be allowed to leave I must get Gene's approval. No manager would give you the OK if your co-worker felt he could not perform his duties if you left. I was very hesitant to confront Gene, but my desire to be with Trina that evening overcame any reservations I had. I realized that the night would be short if I didn't make any room, so I decided to ask Gene if I could leave early.

I said, "Hey buddy (Gene) would it be alright with you if I left early tonight? I pulled a muscle in my back early today and now it's hurting the hell out of me. I want to go home and soak in some hot water to relieve this pain. Do you think you can handle the rest of the evening by yourself?" While asking Gene's permission, I already knew what his answer was going to be. He would love to see me leave because if there were any more guests who needed service, he would be the only beneficiary.

He immediately started laughing and said, "Look Shamar, I don't believe you hurt your back today. The only thing you probably hurt was your eyes from watching that girl who's been coming up here every minute. I know you're trying to hook up with her so go ahead, take the night off." I thanked Gene and went looking for Mr. Gerritzen (Night Manager) to get his permission to check out. This would be my first time leaving work early because I had a mission to accomplish. I never thought a woman would be the reason why I would take off work early.

But this was no ordinary woman; this was a woman that you prayed would come into your life. She had all the qualities that made a man feel confident that he could live a productive life with her. Although I was excited about her, I knew not to move too fast because it could end in disappointment. I concluded to make our dinner date a question and answering period where we could learn more about our past and future goals. I had to keep in mind that this was someone who didn't live in the same city with me and would soon be leaving.

When I finally caught up with Mr. Gerritzen, he was busy dealing with an irate guest who was complaining that his luggage had not arrived to his room after an hour. I was a welcomed sight when Mr. Gerritzen saw me approaching. He immediately waved me over to him and I knew my request to leave early was going to be delayed. He said, "Shamar, this is Mr. Schillings in room 1120. He said his luggage has not yet arrived to his room and I need you to track it down and deliver it. I've already looked in the Bell Closet and it wasn't there. Where else could it be?"

"I have no idea Mr. Gerritzen, but I will give a great deal of effort to find it", I responded. The first thing I did was to take

Mr. Schilling to the Front Desk and ask him to identify who the person was that checked him into the hotel. After pointing out a Guest Agent (Sandra), we both approached her and I asked her did she remember checking in Mr. Schillings. She said sure she remembered him and that he was in room 1120. I asked what Bellman took his luggage up and she said that Charles put the luggage in the office and left to go home for the day.

I immediately went back to retrieve it and brought it out. Mr. Schillings was very delighted to see his luggage and I assisted him back to his room, He said, "Shamar, I can't understand why your Manager didn't take the time to do this. Instead, he dumped my problem into your lap and you responded intelligently. I want to thank you very much and I will be e-mailing your Corporate Headquarters informing them how you went above and beyond to solve my problem. Here's a little something for your troubles." I thanked Mr. Schillings and went looking for Mr. Gerritzen.

I wanted to let him know that I had found Mr. Schillings' luggage and to ask him if I could leave work early. However, I knew he was going to ask where I found Mr. Schillings' luggage. And who was responsible for not getting the luggage to his room? I had to come up with an excuse for Charles because Mr. Gerritzen was very strict and Charles could face some disciplinary action and may lose his job. What he had done was very serious. The rule of the hotel was that you never leave luggage unattended or fail to deliver it to the guest's room in a timely manner. Most guests have meetings and affairs to attend and need their clothes.

Well, what the hell, if Mr. Gerritzen asks me about this incident, I'll just say that it was sitting outside the hotel and someone forgot to bring it into the lobby. Although Charles was a snake sometimes, I couldn't be responsible for him being disciplined. However, the next time I saw him, I would make him aware of the mistake he made. And surely as I assumed he would, Mr. Gerritzen asked me if I found Mr. Schillings' luggage. I gave him the excuse I had concocted for Charles and he was satisfied. I knew his main concern was that no liability occurred on his watch.

I said, "Well Mr. Gerritzen, we have another satisfied guest. Mr. Shillings is in a much better mood. I would like to ask you if I could leave early tonight. Things are slow and Gene said it was alright with him." Mr. Gerritzen just responded by waving bye to me and I exited his office. On my way to my locker, I had to get focused back on the situation at hand and that was my dinner date with Trina. As I rushed to the time clock, my cell phone rang. It was Trina calling to see if our date was still on. This gave me more energy and I rushed home to get dressed for this intimate evening.

Since our hotel was located in the heart of most tourist attractions in the city, I thought I would take Trina to one of the prestigious restaurants downtown. I wanted to make a good impression on her. She surely deserved it. It was something about her that took me out of my comfort zone. Usually when I date a woman, I have my defenses up on the first date. I know that I'm looking for a special woman to share my life, one that I must feel a bond with. Recently, I haven't been successful. My choices wind up being disappointments with the woman being too materialistic.

Anyway, I called Trina and asked her to meet in front of Club Elite, which was one block from the hotel. As I was standing there, I could see her exiting the hotel looking stunning. I greeted her with a nice gentle hug and we proceeded to The Lighthouse. This was a restaurant located on the top floor of the Paramount Suites, a thirty-story luxury suite apartment building with a giant search light on top simulating a lighthouse. The décor of the restaurant was very elaborate and expensive. The food was savory and we enjoyed the evening.

After enjoying my dinner and conversation with Trina, we both concluded that we must continue our relationship. We didn't make any obligations instead we agreed to stay in contact and try to see if we were compatible with each other. So I walked her back to the hotel and proceeded home for the night. I realized that she would be going home to New Mexico in a couple of days. The KAK Convention would be ending and our communication would be long distance. I could not dwell on the thought of her leaving because we had just met and I must let time take its course.

Bad Judgments

After returning to work the next day, I was met with news that management was waiting for Gene and I to arrive so that we could have a meeting. I had not quite made it to the Café before I was interrupted by Charles. He said, "Hey man, what happened last night after I left work? Sandra (Front Desk Agent) told me that Mr. Gerritzen was tripping about a guest not getting his luggage right away. She said he was giving you shit about it. What did he say man?" I couldn't answer him right away, so I continued to the Café. I was disgusted with him because he caused the trouble.

I didn't know what Charles was thinking about not delivering a guest's luggage to his room. Anyway, whatever the meeting was about I wasn't worried. Charles was the bad Bellman of the hotel and everyone knew that. His personal problem and inconsistencies caused him to make bad judgments on the job. My only thought now was to grab something to eat before I clocked in. Like I said, our hotel was like Peyton Place and every department had its issues. When you come to the Employees Café, you hear all the rumors that are circulating.

Whether it's good news or bad, a story of an employee usually gets twisted into controversy. As I finished my lunch, I headed to the lobby to start my day. Upon my arrival, I was directed to Mr. Gentry's office for the meeting with all the Bellmen. Everyone in the room seemed to be on edge except me. I had learned not to worry about anything you have no control over. My mindset was that I hadn't done anything wrong and was unaware of the situation at hand. As I sat down next to Charles, he nervously said, "After this meeting Shamar, I'm going to tell you what happened last night."

Mr. Gentry entered the room and announced he had a task for us to perform. It was the day before the KAK Convention was to end. Their President wanted some notices delivered to each member's room that night. Since they occupied some six hundred rooms, he wanted us to divide the deliveries equally among us.

"Listen guys, here's a chance for all of you to make some good money. I told the President that it would be four dollars for each room and she concurred. Be sure that you knock on the door hard before you enter to deliver the notices.

The last time we had a big drop like this; there were problems with the Bellmen being in a hurry to get through with their rooms and entering without knocking. Please guys, I don't want any complaints about anyone walking in on guests undressed or sleeping…If there is a DND (Do Not Disturb) sign on the door, just leave the packet at the door. Are there any questions? If not, Gene will have a list of all the rooms and I don't want anyone clocking out until everyone has completed this task," he said.

After the meeting, everyone gave a big sigh of relief. This meant that all of us would be earning an extra five-hundred dollars on our checks. Everyone was excited and anxious to get started. Gene asked me to go with him to the delivery dock to pick-up the boxes to be delivered. Without hesitation, Rick and Precious volunteered to make copies of the order in which we would proceed. After getting our packages and list of rooms, Charles pulled me inside the Bell-Closet and said, "Shamar, I thought that meeting was going to be about the incident last night…."

I immediately interrupted him from continuing, because it was time for business and we had to get the packages delivered. I told him that after we completed our job, we could sit down and discuss the matter. The discussion before the meeting was that we were going to get scolded for losing Mr. Schillings' luggage that previous night, but the incident was never mentioned by Mr. Gentry. His only concern was that we work together to get the Drop done. "Drop" was a phase we used in the hotel industry to describe a delivery to guests' rooms.

The Drop was going perfectly and everyone was on time with their deliveries. It was a shock that I was the Bellman who had room 842 on my list. This was Trina Jones' room and I made it my business to make her my last delivery. I knew that after today, she would be checking out and going back to New Mexico. The thought of her leaving weighed heavy on my heart because I hadn't completed the bond I wanted with her. I could only imagine some other man would see the beauty and love that she was willing to share. She was the perfect woman for me, but she could be walking out of my life.

As I approached Trina's room, I knocked and identified myself twice. There was no answer so I entered her room with my passkey and left her package on the bed. As I was leaving, I saw her getting off the elevator. "Hi Shamar, you're looking for me? I just left the front desk looking for you….they said that you were making some Drops. I just wanted to see if we could get together before I leave tomorrow. Are you busy when you get off tonight? I want to take you out for a drink," she said. She did not realize that this was what I was hoping for.

I gave her a big kiss and hug and said, "Hi baby, I would be delighted to have a drink with you after work. I wanted so much to be with you before you departed for home. I have something that I would like to discuss with you anyway. It's going to be a good night. So look, just meet me at Club Elite around 10:30 PM and I'll be expecting you." I got a sensual smile from her as she said, "Okay baby, I'll be there. Have a good evening." As we departed company, I could not help but to watch her strut back to her room with that big ass.

As we finished with our Drop, all the Bellmen were full of enthusiasm. While we had a break, I thought that this would be a good time to finish my conversation with Charles. I couldn't imagine what was so important, but I knew that he respected me as a Leader and always asked for my advice on certain issues. However, the realization was that everyone had made four dollars for each Drop. This was going to look good in their checks. Six of us had participated and that's about four-hundred fifty dollars per Bellman. The excitement had died down, so Charles and I slipped into the Bell-Closet.

Charles started off by saying, "Thanks man for not flipping on me regarding the incident last night. After Mr. Schillings checked in, he approached me with an offer I could not refuse. He wanted me to find him a hit of crack for fifty dollars. After I brought it back to him, he was going to give me fifty dollars. That's why I put his luggage in the back office. Here's twenty-five dollars for looking out for me." I looked at him in disbelief, but accepted the twenty-five dollars. The only thing I said was that he should be careful doing something like that.

After evaluating the dilemma, I could not blame Charles for making a quick fifty bucks for doing something he was comfortable with. You see, that was his life. He was involved deeply in drugs and that environment. He knew exactly when and where drugs were available, since he was dependent upon them. Everyone in the hotel knew of his transgressions except Management. I always wondered how he passed the drug screening for employment. However, that was not my concern because Charles was always polite and professional with the guests. You would never think that he was on drugs.

Anyway, I assured Charles that I would not mention this incident to anyone, but told him not to disclose any more adventures he had with guests. I do not want to be a conspirator or have any knowledge of what could be a criminal act. Although the guests that I check in to the hotel all have faults in their lives, as does everyone else, we as public servants must maintain a standard above that. I left Charles with that thought and stressed to him that it could been a setup.

Although Charles had violated the moral character of the hotel and its employees, every guest checks into the hotel with different objectives:

Work: Commuters who stay at the hotel weekly
Conventions: Religious Groups, Sororities, Business
Business Meetings: Worldwide companies, Local groups

Conferences: Companies, Introductions, Socialization

Weddings: Usually Guests and Family from out of town

Training Workshops: Lectures and Knowledge info

Seminars: Students/employees doing research

Pleasure: Tourists, Special Events, etc.

Criminal: Illegal Intentions

The last is the one you're never prepared for. Some people use hotels as transfer points for several illicit activities.

After my conversation with Charles, it was time to get back to work. We had completed our Drops and there was only two hours left in my day. Suddenly I was called by Guests Response to go check a guest out of room 1512. Upon my arrival I was surprised that the guest was not checking out. He wanted me to store a small suitcase in our Bell-Closet. I told the guest that I would get him a claim ticket so he could retrieve his bag. However, this request was unusual because we usually store luggage when guests have late checkouts or late fights.

This was not the case with room 1512. I checked his reservation and he wasn't checking out for another three days. When I took the claim ticket back to his room, he had a suspicious looking character in his room. I handed him his ticket and he tipped me ten dollars. As I left the room, I realized that the shady character was someone that I recognized. He was a guy named Daniel Snider who had spent twenty years in

Federal Prison for Drug Trafficking. Although he grew up in my hood, I hadn't seen him in years.

Anyway, it wasn't my concern what was going on in 1512, but I knew it was very suspicious that they wanted a bag stored. I didn't let my curiosity get the best of me, so I focused back on meeting with Trina that evening. After clocking out for the day, I hurried home to get ready for my date at Club Elite. I had just bought a new suit and shoes that would surely turn heads toward me. I would be remiss if I hadn't stopped to buy a nice 'Thinking of You' card to present to Trina along with flowers.

Upon my arrival, Trina was already seated at a table with a tablecloth, adorned with a bucket of Moët and candles. I thought how classy it was, since no other table in the club adorned such a glow, especially with the finest woman there. My first words to Trina after my presentation, was how did she know that Moët was my favorite champagne? She said, "Well baby, while requesting this special table, the guy who was getting it ready asked me who I was expecting. I told him your name and a big smile came across his face. He said don't worry beautiful lady; I'll take care of you. I didn't order the Moët. He brought it over."

I immediately thought that someone was being flirtatious because she had come in alone. It was not unusual that a guy would send a single woman a bucket of champagne. A lot of high rollers hang out at the club. A hundred bucks wasn't anything to pay for a chance to catch a bad bitch.

"Trina, who was the guy that sent you this Moët, because I want to give him his money back", I said. She looked around the club for a while and finally said, "Baby, there he is – the guy with the beard." As I turned around to look – it was the owner of the club giving me a thumbs-up!!! I felt relieved because he was a good friend of mine and was just making things right for me. I gave him a right-on sign and continued my attention with Trina. We spent the evening conversating about our lives. We ended by making a commitment to continue seeing each other once a month by alternating our travel.

After a delightful evening with Trina, I realized that this was our last encounter for a while. She would be checking out early the next morning while I was sleeping. I wanted so badly to have sex with her but I didn't want to ruin the chemistry we had created. The physical and moral attraction you have for someone has to be balanced. You see, my zodiac sign is Libra (the scales) and we weigh every decision we make. I've been looking for a woman who I could spend the rest of my life with that had a meaningful purpose. Trina seemed to be the one and I planned to hold on to her.

I was assured by Trina that she was excited about our brief encounter and wanted so much to see how serious we both could make our relationship work. We ended our night with a walk back to the hotel. I wished her a safe and pleasurable flight home. She grabbed me by the ass as if she was requesting pleasure, but I knew it was the same passion I was feeling. Our minds were thinking lust but we abstained from the physical pleasure that only would have lasted briefly. We released each other and left with a kiss.

I went home that night with the thought of another guest who I had an encounter with, Ms. D. Although she was gone, I still received affectionate e-mails from her. My tenure as a Bellman has been met with several challenges. Whether they are moral or immoral, women visit hotels with a thirst for attention. Now don't get me wrong, I know businesswomen come for meetings, work, vacations, etc., but you have a small percentage that are lonely and have no significant other in their life to fulfill their desires.

Anyway, my evening with Trina was meaningful and I promised to keep it adventurous.

As I awakened the next day thinking only of tips that I would be making from the KAK checkout, it would surely be a profitable day because these ladies were very generous. When I arrived at work, the Lobby was flourishing with guests and luggage everywhere. The luggage closet was filled to capacity and a line of guests extended to the front door. I could not help but notice that the guest in room 1512 was standing in line to get the bag I had checked in for him.

I had immediately gotten busy going to guests' rooms retrieving their luggage so that they could depart the hotel. After several trips to rooms, the guest in room 1512 acted as if he was trying to get my attention. I finally asked him if there was something he needed. He said, "Listen Bellman, I see you all have a lot of people checking out. I also see a lot of luggage going in and out of your storage. I gave you a bag to store for me and I don't want it to get lost in the shuffle, so please check to see if it's still there."

After taking his claim ticket, I checked and his bag was still where I had put it. I informed him that his bag was there and handed his ticket back to him. "Thank you Bellman, I appreciate that very much. I know you all are busy, but please make sure my bag doesn't disappear. Here's ten dollars for your troubles." I gave him my gratitude and assured him that I would make sure his bag wouldn't get away. Again, his actions seemed suspicious because he still was in the company of this well-known drug dealer. Much attention was given to his bag.

While the KAK Sorority was checking out, we had a group of J.P. Morgan executives waiting to check in to start their conference the next day. Rooms were not ready and Housekeeping was working overtime to keep up the pace. Luggage was being stored in every available space behind the Front Desk.

This was the busiest I had ever seen the hotel. As soon as a Bellman came down with a guest, there's another guest waiting with a claim-ticket to retrieve or store their luggage. The M.O.D. (Manager On Duty) was assisting in all areas.

The greatest relief came when all the Sorority members were finally checked out. Now the task was to get all the other guests who were waiting, up to their rooms as the rooms became available. Our GM (Mr. Sutter) was even pushing carts to and from guest rooms. The atmosphere of the hotel was jovial because all the staff had come together to help each other get the guests serviced. Although service was slow, I did not see one disappointed guest. Everyone was patient and polite. This response gave me a great sense of pride, which made for a good day.

As the day began to wind down, everyone was giving each other hugs for a job well done. I had never seen the staff in such a caring moment. Everyone had worked very hard to ensure that the company's motto was lived up to, "TO SERVICE AND PROVIDE THE NEEDS OF OUR GUESTS."

All the Bellmen were in private areas counting their tips. I had personally made six-hundred dollars in tips. This could not have been a better day, especially with everyone in harmony. However, we had handled around three-thousand pieces of luggage and the exhaustion was evident in everyone. When we did get a break, I noticed Gene nodding off to sleep in the Bell-

Closet. I tipped up on him and gave a loud shout that made him jump with fear. Everyone was laughing, but Gene did not think it was funny. He stormed out of the Bell-Closet and headed toward the elevator while looking back at me in anger. I knew it was going to be an eventful day between us two. Gene did not like me and this added more resentment to our relationship.

Anyway, another adventurous day was ending for me. I left the hotel thinking of room 1512. I didn't know why I felt strange about dealing with this guest, but my suspicions never failed me. Throughout my life I was gifted with the ability to read people's thoughts and intentions. What made a red flag come up was the attention he was giving to the bag I had stored for him in the Bell-Closet. Having Daniel Snider in his room (The convicted drug dealer) did not contribute to his credibility as a legitimate guest.

I shook all the negative thoughts I was having and focused on the money I had made in tips. My front pockets had the mumps and I couldn't wait to count my receipts. As I headed to turn my passkey into Security, I noticed that several Federal Agents were talking to the Head of our Security team. One of the team members had told me in the locker room that they had an unexpected visit from the DEA but wasn't quite sure what was going on. This situation heightened my suspicion of room 1512, but I didn't give it another thought.

As I arrived home for the evening, I laid in bed thinking what had transpired at work. Usually I count my tips before I leave the hotel, but I emptied my pockets on my bedroom floor and began counting. It was a very profitable day. I realized how blessed I've been to land a job in an industry where you can earn tax-free money. I mean you're required to report your tips to the IRS, but how do they know how much you made…? Keep in mind that Bellmen do not earn a hefty salary- much less than minimum wage, but their tips compensate for loss of salary. I went to sleep that night anticipating the influx of guests arriving for another Convention. I also had a bad feeling that the hotel would experience a breach of security. This was a result of seeing a look of concern on Mr. Mullins' face (Chief of Security) while talking with the DEA agents. He seemed to be very nervous as well as surprised while speaking to them. All these thoughts gave me enough comfort to fall into a deep sleep.

Awakening the next day was a poor man's dream. Knowing that if you made it through the day; you would come home with at least two-hundred dollars in your pocket. As I got dressed for work, I could not help but reflect on the previous day's events.

Upon my arrival at work, I noticed an Officer leaving the Delivery Dock with a Drug Sniffing dog. When I entered the employee entrance to pick up my passkey, the Security Officers had concerned looks on their faces. I continued to the Staff Café so that I could hear what was going on in "Peyton Place." I was barely inside when Precious approached. "Hey Shamar! The Feds just left our Bell-Closet with Drug Sniffing Dogs... Management had all of us stand outside the hotel until they finished. I don't know what the fuck is going on; do you think somebody planted a bomb in this motherfucker?" I couldn't do anything but bust out laughing at her. I said, "Well baby, whatever's going on, I'm sure we'll know about it momentarily. Mr. Gerritzen will be calling a meeting before today is over."

And surely as I arrived in the lobby to begin working, a short meeting was called in Mr. Gerritzen's office. I glanced around the lobby and everything seemed normal. Guests were checking in and luggage was being taken to their rooms. The flow of the traffic was heavy because it was another Convention starting that day. Everyone was so busy we could not hold the meeting. Although there was something wrong internally, we as Bellmen could not focus on a dilemma that would interfere with us servicing the guests.

As the day went by, I kept noticing unfamiliar men hanging around elevators and the Bell-Closet. This was very unusual because none of the other Bellmen knew them or their purpose for posting up in the lobby. When someone asked them if they needed assistance, they would only reply that they were waiting for someone to come down from their room. This response was common because guests do wait to gather before they leave for meetings, dinner, cocktails, etc., so I continued working without a second thought.

While waiting at the front entrance of the hotel, I noticed a fabulously dressed young lady walk to the Check-in counter and ask the clerk to dial room 1512. The clerk dialed the room and handed the woman the phone. "Hello baby, how are you doing? I'm in the lobby of the hotel," she said. She gave a long pause before giving the phone back to the clerk. She continued to the elevator to go up to 1512. He was the shady character whose bag I had stored in the Bell-Closet. I immediately went back to see if the bag was still there and it was.

After an hour had passed, I encountered the two of them on the elevator as I was taking a cart of luggage down for a guest who was checking out. With excitement in his eyes, the guest in 1512 said, "Hey Bellman, what's up? I'm glad I saw you. I'm on my way down to pick up the bag you stored for me a few days ago. Here's my claim ticket. Give the bag to her while I go check out."

As we arrived in the lobby, the guest who I was assisting, led me to a waiting Town Car which was taking him to the airport. I hurriedly loaded his luggage into the trunk of the car and went straight to the Bell-Closet, where the young lady with the guest in 1512 was waiting. I pilfered a glance at the Checkout Counter and noticed a new face checking the guest in 1512 out. I didn't give it a second thought because Front Desk

Agents are hired constantly. For some reason it was a big turnover in this position. Anyway, I proceeded to get his bag.

Little did I know that I was handling four kilos of pure heroin that had been in a safe place before 1512 decided to move it. While handing the young lady his bag, the guest in 1512 approached and took possession of it while handing me a ten-dollar tip. As he turned to exit the hotel, five DEA Agents rushed over and grabbed him and the lady. They both were cuffed and led out the side door. The man who was checking him out of the hotel came over and swooped the bag off the floor. It was surprising to find out that he also was an Agent impersonating a Front-Desk Clerk.

After this episode had ended, everyone in the lobby had opened mouths at what just happened. Everything happened so fast that some people didn't notice the drama that had taken place. I realized that the DEA had everything planned. This is the reason why so many strange people were hanging out in the lobby (Agents). They didn't want the guest in 1512 to escape and they had to actually see him with the goods in his hand. While growing up in a crime-ridden area of the city, I had never actually witnessed a real sting operation. It was amazing because I was unaware that I would be playing a role in it.

I could not do anything but reminisce on the suspicion that I had of today's event. Evidently, the dogs were used to confirm that there were drugs in the bags. After that, they posted up to see who would retrieve the bags. It even made me realize why Daniel Snider was in his room when I stored the bag. Remember, Mr. Snider was the guy I knew as a convicted drug dealer. After gossip circulated throughout the hotel, another day ended in the life of a Bellman.

The Grandeur

GRANDEUR: Splendor, great size, beauty. This was a great name for our hotel. Its definition describes the atmosphere when you walk into the lobby. While taking up one city block, it also stood twenty-five stories tall with twelve hundred rooms!

Reminiscing about the day I stumbled into the hotel to apply for a job as a Bellman, I never imagined that it would be delightful as it was. The mere thought of earning five-dollars and fifty cents per hour was inconceivable at that time. That was only two hundred twenty dollars a week before taxes. There was no way possible that a grown man could survive on that salary. Anyway, I didn't have to survive on that because I was never dependent on my paycheck. My survival has been dependent on tips – while my check was direct-deposited every week. However, it wasn't the money that excited me. It was the pleasure of greeting and conversating with people of different nationalities. Our hotel was multi-cultural and guests' needs and desires were met regardless.

Time went by quickly and it has been over a year since I was hired as Bellman. That was an accomplishment because now I was eligible to use my acquired vacation time. Until then, I was only able to take weekend flights to visit Trina in Albuquerque New Mexico. Now it was time to be more adventurous and spend a week somewhere....The only thing I enjoyed about visiting New Mexico was the weather. With a population of 2.3 million and the highest percentage of Hispanics made it a state without much tourism.

Anyway, until I decided when and where I was going to take a vacation, it was another dilemma I had to meet on my job.

Since I've been in my position, there have been several Management and Staff changes in the hotel. Managers are always looking to change hotels for higher positions. Our hotel was a Fortune 500 Company/NYSE with over $15 billion in revenue. We hand over twelve different brands with more than 3,000 locations in 70 countries.

With change so massive, it was a great opportunity for one to advance or transfer to another region. My tenure at the Grandeur has been met with great expectations. Although I had established myself as the best Bellman, there was another job they wanted me to do.

As I came in to work, Phil (Doorman) approached and said, "Hi Shamar, I told Mr. Gerritzen that I would be taking a 90-day leave to have a hernia operation. He told me to ask if you were willing to be cross-trained to work the door until I recuperate. It wouldn't make sense for them to hire someone, besides, I get tipped more then you Bellman...I suggested you because you have more personality than the others. On a good day you would make at least two-hundred dollars in tips."

The opportunity to be a Doorman has always been appetizing to me. The Doorman is the first person a guest encounters upon their arrival to the hotel. The Doorman is the diplomat of the hotel and provides the most service for guest's needs. Your charm and smile is measured by how much money you can earn.

After evaluating the percentage of daily occupancy of the hotel (50-60%), I realized that we were in our slow season. Hotels have low and peak seasons when guests don't travel much. Usually this occurs during the months of November, December, and January and until Spring. Geographically our hotel was located where we received four seasons (Spring, Summer, Fall and Winter). Making tips during the holiday season was bad for Bellmen, so I didn't give it a second thought when I had the opportunity to be a Doorman.

I immediately informed Mr. Gerritzen that I would accept his offer for me to replace Phil upon his departure. Although the position was temporary, it was alluring because the Doorman's salary was two dollars more per hour than the Bellmen. So I was reclassified as a Bellman/Doorman, which entitled me to receive the pay increase. Of course, this change did not sit very well with the other Bellmen. They all contested the fact that I didn't have seniority over them to be considered for the position. However, I did feel somewhat guilty because they were here before me and weren't given the opportunity.

Mr. Gerritzen had a meeting with all the Front-Office Staff to announce my new duties. Although he was getting heated discussions about choosing me over the other Bellmen, he remained calm. After listening to all the haters, he ended the meeting by saying, "Listen, I understand your being upset, but realistically, who's the best Bellman among you...? Shamar!!! He has demonstrated his professionalism. He received our SPIRIT TO SERVE Guest award. Some of you have been here over ten years and haven't been awarded anything but longevity."

Everyone in the meeting got quiet and hung their heads. Mr. Gerritzen ended the meeting by telling them that his decision was final and if they didn't like it, they could turn in their resignations. I was surprised, but proud. I didn't realize that Management felt so proud of me. I left the meeting with the other Bellman being apologetic to me. I got them all together and said, "Hey guys don't be hating on me. I didn't ask them for the job. They approached me and offered it. Now let's put this behind us and continue doing what's expected of us."

A week had passed since our meeting and everything was back to normal. It seemed that everyone was comfortable with my transition. Phil was in the hospital having his operation and I was enjoying every moment of filling his shoes. I didn't have a hard time doing that, but it was more physical because I had to unload all guests' luggage from their cars, shuttles, limos, taxis, etc. After loading the Bell-Cart, I had to Valet their vehicles, if they were driving. Then I had the tasks of pulling their luggage into the lobby to the Check-in Counter.

It's usually at curbside when I present myself. I would say, "Hello, my name is Shamar, welcome to the fabulous Grandeur Hotel. I would be delighted to unload your vehicle and get your car safely parked in our secured garage, where you have in and out privileges upon your request." Sometimes I would change my greetings depending who I observed in the vehicle. If it's a family with children, I would acknowledge them first. Parents usually feel welcome when you give their children attention. When a bright smile comes over their faces, you are almost promised a tip.

It took a few days before I was able to handle my new duties with confidence. Being a doorman was challenging because you provided so many services for guests. Hailing taxis was time-consuming and required a lot of patience. Guests would gather outside the hotel going to dinner and meetings. Usually it was when everyone was getting off work and the taxis were servicing numerous hotels in the area, which made it difficult to get one. This task was often greatly rewarded because most guests gave you a tip for getting them a taxi.

Some guests have a party of six or seven that requires limo services. This is when you get handsomely rewarded because not only did the guests tip you, the Taxi Driver would give you a stipend for calling him. You also get a stipend from Limo and Town Car runs to the airport.

The tips for Doormen were unlimited. Even calling the Valet vehicles in front of the hotel was met with tips, which I kindly shared with the Valet man. Giving directions and recommending fine dining was sometimes met with courtesy.

The Grandeur was definitely a fast paced hotel with different activities going on at once, especially when there's a big convention. Usually there are two or three workshops going on, along with meetings, lectures, etc. All of the breakfast rooms would be occupied by different groups discussing their objectives. It was a pleasure being in such an enterprising atmosphere. This brought about huge rewards for all the hotel employees. From Bellmen to Housekeeper, everyone was given tips for their services.

This was truly a Five Star Hotel! This title is given to any luxury hotel that provides all the amenities that guests need to be comfortable. Everything was at your disposal at the Grandeur:

- Swimming Pool
- Jacuzzi
- Gift Store
- Concierge Lounge & Services
- Wine Bar
- Cocktail Lounge
- Starbucks Coffee Shop
- FedEx® Store
- 2 Restaurants
- Hertz Rental Car

Several weeks had passed since I started my duties as a Doorman. The Doorman's obligation was to stand posted outside the hotel regardless of weather conditions. Although the hotel provided clothing for all seasons, the rain was never appreciated. You get very familiar with all the activities and people that pass by you every day, especially the business of the hotel. Deliveries are constantly made to the hotel daily and that included mail, UPS and FedEx® packages, lost guests' luggage from the airports, etc.

The main visit we received was from Brinks. They would come weekly to pick up the hotel's receipts. The hotel also provided a seasonal Shoeshine Booth for guests outside the hotel during warm climates. The booth was operated by a close friend who I had started school with. Although he had moved out of town for a while, we rekindled our friendship while working outside the hotel every day. We would often converse about old times growing up, while standing around.

One day Joe (Shoeshine Man) and I decided to stop and have dinner when we both got off work. We hadn't spent any time together since we were kids and it was overdue.

Joe said, "Hey Shamar, let's stop at 'Sam's Crab Shack', I got a taste for some of those good ole crab cakes. I want you to have an open mind because there's something important I need to discuss with you."

I became startled for a moment because the last person that said that to me was Charles. The conversation with him involved some drama I wasn't happy with. Anyway I didn't let his statement be a negative factor on our anticipated appetite for some good food. Besides, Joe did not have the mentality of Charles. He appeared to be more grounded and wanted to be more than a Shoeshine boy. Judging by the conversations we had, he believed that he wasted his life doing nothing to prepare for his future. Now in his fifties, he felt that life was getting short. His desire was to find something that would enrich his life instantly.

After getting off work that evening, Joe and I met at the time-clock and proceeded to have dinner at 'Sam's Crab Shack'. His whole discussion was about how he had been noticing the habits of the Brinks truck when it came to the hotel every week.

Although I was an opportunist and had taken chances in life to make a fast buck, I had gotten older and jail wasn't an option now. I knew where Joe was going with this conversation because I also had been watching how careless the Brinks driver was when picking up the hotel's receipts. We both worked outside the hotel and were aware of all scheduled deliveries.

While being seated at the restaurant, Joe said, "I've been thinking about knocking that Brinks truck off. All it takes is a little planning and it can be a piece of cake. I've been watching their habits for a month now. Since I'm posted outside the hotel when they go in, I need someone to tell me how the driver moves once he gets the cash from the safe. That's where you come in. I know you see all his moves inside. Just think about it before you answer."

I just stared at Joe in amazement, unable to say anything for a while. However, I could not help but think while working as a Bellman I would see the Brinks driver come through the Bell-Closet door and walk down the corridor to the Cash Office. This office served as a place for check-cashing, exchanging denominations, and deposits for all department receipts. I thought about all the cash the hotel takes in on a weekly basis. The thought was tempting, but I had to be realistic about our chance of pulling off a perfect robbery.

I immediately snapped out of the negative thoughts I was having and responded to Joe, "Hey dude, that's heavy. How long have you been planning this, or is it just a thought?"

"No man, I'm serious about this. Just let me tell you my plan and then give me an answer", he said.

I wasn't listening because the only thing I saw was jail. At fifty-five years of age, I knew I wouldn't live through a long prison term. Anyway, my life wasn't bad working at the hotel. My income was more than the Manager's salaries.

As I mentioned before, the hotel was very profitable and maintained enough guests for a Bellman/Doorman to make a good living. The cost of living was very economical in the state where I lived. It didn't appear that my job was threatened by our cutbacks or buyouts, so I felt confident that I was secure in my position. However, my mind did tell me to at least listen to Joe's plan to see if it could be pulled off. So, to end the conversation, I told Joe to give me a few days to think about it.

We continued our dinner laughing and talking about our childhood. It was a relief for me to have this time with Joe because he was adventurous as well as academically inclined. This was why I listened to Joe's rich scheme to rob the Brinks' truck. Although I hadn't heard his plan, I knew he wasn't stupid enough to do something that wasn't possible. All through our childhood, I remembered how he used to calculate every mischievous thing he did.

Anyway, our dinner was over and we left the restaurant. I went home evaluating everything Joe had discussed with me about the robbery. Although I had a nice savings from my tips, it was not enough for all the things I needed and desired. Sometimes greed sets in when you wish for materialistic comfort. I realized that it was time for me to relax and erase all the negative thoughts Joe had brought to my mind.

I went to work the next day realizing that it had been a couple of months since my tenure as a Doorman. It was just a few weeks left before Phil would return to his position. The hotel was still in its slow season and no Conventions were immediately scheduled. We were just relying on our weekly working guests and daily check-ins. The average tip for taking guests up to their rooms was five bucks, but when there's no activity you're lucky to get two bucks. Frustration sets in when you get stiffed (No tip). That's when you're ready to leave work early.

The Grandeur was an amazing hotel to work for. We were a new hotel (5 years) that replaced two previous ones, or should I say we bought the hotels out.

The 'Statler' was the first hotel in our location. It was built in 1936. I remembered shining shoes in front of the hotel when I was a youth. My friends and I would find scrap wood to build a shoeshine box. I was amazed by the ornate structure of the building that attracted the rich and famous people who visited our city. It was always a glamorous place that showcased the downtown area.

Over the years the Statler was replaced by 'Stouffer's Hotels' who maintained the five-star status it had previously been known for. Then came 'The Grandeur', who demolished the building that was adjacent to Stouffers and built an adjoining hotel to make it the largest one in the city. When you entered The Grandeur, you would realize that the two buildings connected. The décor was the same throughout.

As I mentioned before, The Grandeur employees were multicultural and that included several ethnic heritages. Our staff consisted of Asians, Latinos, African-Americans, Vietnamese, etc. Most of the employees were grandfathered in from the previous hotel and had thirty years seniority. Their longevity made it difficult for some employees to get full-time hours. The Employee Café always was diverse in their menu selections to accommodate everyone's cuisine.

The hotel's Corporate Office always recognized quality services that an employee provided to their guests. A comment card was provided in every guest's room for them to rate the service they received. When taking guests to their rooms, we are required to give them an orientation of the hotel and all service and amenities they're entitled to. The concierge lounge was only available for Elite Members, who earned points through their visits. It was located on the Penthouse Level where there was a view of the river and entire city. It was a breath-taking view while enjoying your meal in a tranquil atmosphere.

Anyway, weeks went by and it was Phil's day to return to work. As I picked up my duties as a Bellman, everyone's (Bell Staff) attitude seemed to have changed. I had received an award for "Outstanding Service" and I felt that it was some jealousy among them.

Things went on as usual and I was treated as an outcast by the other Bellmen. Although I had been working with these guys for over a year, I became disgusted with their attitudes. I knew I hadn't done anything to them, but they were acting as if I did.

Phil had noticed the change of feelings toward me. He said, "Listen Shamar, don't let them get you upset. Its part of the Bellman's game. They're all mad at you because you were chosen to hold my job down while I was gone. They saw you making money while there were no Fronts coming in."

What Phil was saying made a lot of sense. I took their attitudes with a grain of salt and continued doing my job. I knew it would end eventually.

The Robbery

Things were not getting better between me and the other Bellmen. Months had passed and our communication wasn't here anymore. The respect for each other diminished and the atmosphere was full of tension. There were incidents where I wasn't called when it was my turn to get a Front. The worst disappointment came when guests would call the Bell Stand and request my service to come get their luggage. When the guests arrived in the lobby with another Bellman, the guests would tell me that they had called for me!

Day after day, conflict would constantly increase with each incident getting more scandalous. Not only were they taking my Fronts, they would rush guests who were retrieving their luggage from storage. This service always warranted a tip and would accumulate after several trips. I even let my frustration be known by approaching them, letting them know that I wasn't going to let them take advantage of me. It wasn't that they knew I was "soft"; they were trying to provoke me into doing something stupid. This tactic is known as "smoking a person out!!!" They had conspired with each other to isolate me so I could not make more money than them. Their hatred of my social skills was always prevalent from the day I started work with them. However, I had to figure out a way to subdue their aggressiveness because I was thinking of physical retaliation. I never thought I would feel this way about them, but listen, they were stopping my money.

The turning point came when a guest was approaching me with her claim-ticket to retrieve her luggage. From out of nowhere, Charles intercepted the ticket and proceeded to the Bell-Closet. I immediately followed him inside and grabbed him by the neck. "Listen Motherfucker!!!! Don't you ever disrespect me like that. You saw that guest approaching me. I'm not going to have you taking money out of my pocket, bitch," I said.

The only thing he could do was release the ticket out of fright and gasp for breath. This episode with Charles left me breathless. I was trembling with nervousness, not knowing how it was going to end. I hurriedly grabbed the guest's luggage and gave it to her. I rushed back to the Bell-Closet to check on Charles, he had left. I assumed that he was on his way to the Manager's office to report me.

I knew it was automatic dismissal for violently striking another employee. I just succumbed to the fact that they had accomplished their goal of getting me fired. They had outwitted me, I thought. I couldn't deny it because there was a security camera in the Bell-Closet. "SHIT!!! I'm gone."

Well, it was nothing I could do but accept the fact that I had fucked up....My mentality is that you can't control anything that's meant to happen. It's just the same if you contract an illness that's untreatable...What can you do??? However, I do believe in KARMA (Destiny). If you mistreat or do wrong to someone, eventually it will come back at you.

I went home that evening considering leaving the hotel. I was so frustrated. I was thinking of the environment I was living in. It was my childhood home that my mother never left. I was forced back there because my mother was alone and getting older, experiencing illness and physical disabilities. However, she was a headstrong woman from the old school who felt comfortable in the neighborhood in which she raised her family.

Although I had left that community some forty years ago, I felt comfortable because all the old heads were still there. Some of my childhood friends never had the inspiration to look past the ghetto. "Ghetto" is just a figure of speech. It was by no means a place without heat or hot water. Nor was it a community of decaying buildings and rats, but a government subsidized housing complex called, 'THE PROJECTS'.

With all these thoughts in my mind, I knew realistically that if I decided to transfer to another city, I had to have enough money to provide for my mother and me. I could not leave her alone.

My mind was racing as I lay down to sleep that night. I didn't know what to expect the next day after choking Charles. When I left work, I wasn't approached by any of the Managers. Charles was nowhere around and the last person I saw was Precious. She said, "Shamar, Charles told me that you attacked him and he's pissed off. The last words I heard him say was he's going to get that motherfucker!!! You better be careful and watch you back."

I knew it was a threat but I didn't let it worry me. I swore that if this incident didn't get me fired, I was going to leave the Grandeur. Although I had saved several thousand dollars, it was vanishing quickly because of my mother and my expenses. Rent, utilities, medicine, food, clothing, etc. was only possible through the tips I made at work. If not for my tips, there was no way possible I could sustain our household. It would lower our standard of living. I had to think of a B-Plan to get my finances together so that I could leave the hotel with some money that would hold us for a while.

The next day I went to work, I walked in the back where the M.O.D.'s offices were. Next to their office was the cashier window where all the hotel's receipts were brought. Employees also cashed their payroll checks there. As I turned around, I bumped into the Brinks bag-man. A quick thought immediately came to my mind, 'Joe.'

I stepped aside to let him by, knowing very well that he was picking up the hotel's receipts. That's my out, I thought!!!

Joe had discussed the desire to rob the Brinks truck, but I didn't want any part of that then. It was evident why I did not consider it because I worked there first and couldn't see it being done without someone taking a chance on getting killed. I never did listen to Joe's plan of carrying it out. I thought that it might be interesting to at least hear Joe out.

As I continued work that day, it was Charles' day off. Everything went normal, serving guests, running errands, and having a good day. No one approached me about the previous day's event. So I started the day in good spirits because the 'CHURCH OF GOD IN CHRIST' was having their national convention and the rooms were sold out. That means that 1,200 guests would be checking in, keeping all the bellmen busy. It didn't matter how much they were hating on me, everyone was going to make big money. These Bishops were known for giving big tips, as much as the KAK ladies, and everyone was focused.

We were so busy that day that I didn't get a chance to speak with Joe. He was busy shining shoes with guests lined up waiting their turn. He was making a bunch of money and as a rule we never interrupted each other while hustling because it could throw you off your 'square.' I decided to call Joe at home that night when we were both off work. I couldn't stop thinking of all the cash the Brinks' bag-man was taking out of the Hotel's safe. I've watched them come and go from the hotel for a year now and never had a negative or devious thought about robbing them until my frustration set in.

Traffic between the hotel and the Convention Center was crowded. Although we were across the street from each other, maneuvering carts with equipment and supplies on them became a challenge. Every time I came out the hotel, Joe gave me a big smile and wink. The Convention was to last ten days and he was marveling in the excitement around the hotel. This was his first year at the hotel and his job was seasonal. It was Fall and this was our last big Convention of the year, meaning he would be laid-off until Spring.

As the evening began to end, I did get a chance to let Joe know that I wanted to get with him after work. He said, "I know buddy...you been thinking about what I said. Look how crowded the hotel is. Man, what I got planned, nobody would ever notice if a robbery went down." I became more excited and anxious wondering how he could carry something like this out without being noticed. My anticipation didn't last too long because our day was over and I was on my way to his house.

While on my way to Joe's house, I began to have doubts about my decision to get involved in something so risky. I knew being subjected to his plan wouldn't let me have an open mind to rationalize if it was possible. All kinds of thoughts were bouncing around in my head and my options were perplexing. I knew I had to relax and calm my nerves; after all, I hadn't made a decision yet.

As I arrived at Joe's house he was already at the door awaiting me. I stepped in and that motherfucker zapped me with a TASER (stun gun). I collapsed to the floor barely conscious, trembling as if I was having a seizure. I must have been incapacitated for at least 30 seconds. The only thing I recalled was hearing his voice apologizing for his actions and saying that he wasn't trying to hurt me. He kept assuring me that I would be alright. As I became alert, he said excitingly, "THIS IS THE PLAN SHAMAR...A ROBBERY WITHOUT A GUN. How do you like it buddy? Nobody gets hurt!! It would be like the snatch /grab we did as kids hustling. Please don't be mad at me, but I had to show you how easy it would be..."

While still trying to recoup from this painful and devious demonstration Joe subjected me to, Joe continued to explain how the TASER affects the sensory and motor functions of the nervous system. It attacks the muscles, causing them to tense up to the point of paralysis (As if I didn't know). Having 10,000 to 30,000 volts go through your body isn't a joke. However, I took his plan as being possible to accomplish with more details, so I sat back to hear more. This was his way to get my attention, but I asked myself, why he needed me?...

I was still upset with him using me as a tester. He wanted to see if the TASER was effective enough to disable the Brinks' bagman while someone grabbed the moneybag from him and quietly disappeared without any attention.

My enthusiasm and confidence in Joe's plan became realistic as he outlined every step of the plan. I realized this wasn't just a quick-get-rich scheme he had concocted frivolously. He had been carefully watching this Brinks truck every time it arrived and knew their schedule. This is what really impressed me and won me over.

Joe and I spent the next two hours discussing the probabilities of fault and the role of each character. My main concern was what role I would be playing. Remember, my complicity was to see if the plan made sense or if I was at risk of being identified as a participant.

Joe said, "Shamar, this is going to be a piece of cake, man. The only role you play is coming out the Valet's entrance after the Brinks man goes in to pick up the cash. My brother is going to sneak in before the door closes and wait until the bagman is ready to leave, zap him with the TASER, grab the bag, and exit the Valet room. Before the bagman regains his composure, my brother would be long gone. The only thing is to get our timing together and we're in there brother... It's going to be sweet like bear meat!!!"

After going over our timing and the position of everyone, the only thing left was to plan a date. I left Joe's house sore and exhausted, but confident we could pull it off. Before leaving, we shook hands and I agreed to participate. We agreed on a trial run before we would actually do it.

When I got home that night I was a little numb from being TASED, but I was convinced that it would be effective in disabling the Brinks' bagman from drawing his firearm. Not only does the TASER affect you physically, but your mind is transcended into confusing thoughts of dying.

So I went to sleep that night reassured I made the right decision. Arriving at work the next day I was met with several challenges. First, I had to apologize to Charles for grabbing him by the neck. He accepted my apology and said, "You know I could have gotten you fired, but I realized that you once covered for me. Now we're even."

After thinking about it, I remembered not snitching him out on something stupid he had done. I was making peace because I knew I had to keep my mind clear of any distractions for the job that lay ahead. I was responsible for planning the point where the Brinks money man gets TASED without too much notice. It was planned that it would be inside the hotel in an isolated place. I had the perfect spot in mind.

You see, the cashier's office was located in the back of the hotel out of sight of anyone except those who worked back there. Traffic was minimal and the corridor led straight to the Valet's room. After entering the Valet's room, there's another door that leads outside the hotel. This is the door the Brinks men enter and leave. A perfect place I thought. If Joe's brother TASED him there it would not be noticed by anyone.

Anyway, tomorrow would be Tuesday, the day the Brinks pickup occurs. I would have a chance to evaluate their every move. They always come at the same time, which makes it easy for me to get posted. Since Joe's shoeshine stand is located outside the Valet entrance, he would have a view of when and where the Brinks truck would park.

With everything in perspective, I continued my day servicing all the arrivals we had. It was the first day of the big Convention and the Bellmen had to assist the Doorman with unloading luggage from vehicles.

Throughout the day we made several trips to the FedEx store to pick up packages for the Bishops that were attending the Convention. Not only did they have a lot of luggage, but some had their clothes shipped in because of the weight and volume. It wasn't unusual for us to pull two loaded carts of luggage to one room. These men of God surely believed in being impressive to their counter-parts. I noticed that some would change suits twice a day, once in the morning and again in the evening while going to their meetings and services. I was amazed at the fashion show I was witnessing. They were clean....

While escorting a guest to her suite, I was interrupted by Joe. He said, "Shamar, look how beautiful it's going to be for us to pull this off without any notice. The hotel is full of people and activities. Let's meet tonight so we can put the final touches on our plan. My brother will be there too, so call me when you get off."

As I got ready to get off work that evening, there were several envelopes handed out to all of the Guest Service employees (Front Office). It was a memo from the GM (General Manager) explaining to the hotel staff that The Grandeur was going to be contracted out under new management to a franchise company. It explained that a meeting would be called for each department to give details and options to current employees. It mentioned that new ownership would occur in ninety days of the date on the memo.

Wow....I thought! I knew exactly what that meant. Motherfuckers were going to lose their jobs because new management had to make way for their employees and they would get first preference. If you couldn't find a sister hotel under our corporation that would hire you, your ass was out!!! Our company didn't have many hotels in the area that would accommodate everyone. We had employees with 20, 30 and 40 years of service that couldn't relocate to other cities. Their obligations were here; home, children, significant other, wife, husbands, etc. This was a no-brainer for them.

Well, with all the events that day, I went home again wondering about my future. Here I was at 56 years of age without a pension or security for the years ahead. Although I felt guilty about committing treason against the hotel that gave me a chance at a job, I knew I wasn't marketable enough to get hired in another position. The pros and cons weighed heavily on my mind and I began to rationalize my decision.

- First: My frustration with the other Bellmen I worked with. Their jealousy and isolation toward me created a negative atmosphere within the hotel and among the guests.
- Second: My complaints to Management were being ignored.
- Third: My financial situation was dependent upon the tips I made. If I did not have the tips, my salary couldn't sustain my cost of living!
- Fourth: I had an ill mother who was dependent on me and the hotel was being sold. It was a chance I wouldn't have a job in 90 days.

After arriving at Joe's house, I explained that the next day (Tuesday) we were going to take positions so that we could see how the Brinks pick-up was made. That is the day the hotel gets paid. However, few employees cashed their checks there.

Anyway there was not much planning to be done. The key to us being successful would be the 'element of surprise'.

Since there would be no gun play or communications, Joe's brother, Zeek, would be the main character. As long as he was positioned in the Valet room when the bagman left the cashier's office, our feat could be accomplished.

We went over several details about what was going to happen after the bagman was incapacitated and the money bag had been grabbed. Everything seemed easy up until that point, but exiting the hotel and what route Zeek was going to take must be flawless. We brain-stormed for several hours until we came to a conclusion. Our main concern was getting away from downtown before any police arrived.

I suggested that we carry out the robbery in one week after we all watched the movements of the pick-up. It would be the day the Convention ended and the hotel would be full of cash.

While on duty, I noticed that most of the guests paid cash for their rooms. This was very unusual; I didn't understand why these churches would lay down thousands of dollars instead of credit cards. Without much insight into this logic, I knew Brinks would be picking up a lot of cash. The Convention would end that Sunday, but the hotel' safe would be full until Tuesday's pick-up.

"Man.... (Thinking out loud), I hope I have enough strength to carry that bag after I take it (laughing)," said Zeek.

He was overjoyed imagining how much money there would be for us to split.

Everything was becoming realistic and the excitement was showing in each of us. We ended the evening sharing stories of what we're going to do with our share. My thoughts were to get on-line and start applying for a job at another hotel because I didn't want to arise any suspicion.

The next day came quickly. The GM had called a meeting in one of our conference rooms to explain more about our demise at The Grandeur in 90 days. Everyone had a grim look on their face as though it was the end of the world. I had never seen the Front Office staff assembled as though they were awaiting their turn at the guillotine.

However, I was in good spirits because I knew in a few days I would have more money than it took to raise me. Everyone else was thinking negative about their future. If the new owners of the hotel didn't have room to hire them, they would be hitting the streets. It was a bitter pill to swallow, but it made you more aware that any event could turn your life around.

We all sometimes take life for granted and don't think about the tragedies we could encounter.

My life was hard growing up and nothing was a surprise to me. I learned to be prepared for any misgivings that happen in your life. After all, I had many of them. This experience made me more determined to take a chance at accomplishing our goal to rob the hotel.

Well The GM came into the Conference room after everyone got through assuming what was going to happen. His entrance and body language was slow and sympathetic.

He said, "Good afternoon everyone...I'm not going to speak long, but I just want to explain your options to secure your jobs. The owners agreed to retain everyone with the highest seniority and experience. The Human Resource department would also be retained and will be contacting all of you within 30 days to let you know if you'll continue working. If you're not chosen, you would have to reapply using the new company's website, as you did when you applied here. Your Department Managers will provide more details on the transition as days go by. I'm willing to answer any questions you have now."

Several people did ask questions but basically the meeting was over. It wasn't too informative because everyone had been briefed by our Union officials of our rights under the contract.

After the meeting, it was close to the time for the Brinks pick-up. Joe and I took our positions to clock the time and movements they made. We only had one week left to actually carry out the robbery and the mental rehearsal was the key to our success. Although we both have been witnessing this pick-up for several months, it was only a wish that we had the contents of that moneybag. Never did I imagine that I would have the motivation or courage to participate in something so risky.

While taking a guest's luggage out to the Doorman, I noticed the Brinks truck pulling up along the side of the hotel out of view of the camera we had in front of the doors (entrance & valet). Joe was already outside because his shoeshine stand was there. I noticed him paying close attention so I went back into the hotel. By the time I entered the back room (offices), I bumped into the bagman entering the corridor going to the cashier's office. I excused myself and we both apologized.

The surprising observation I got was that the bagman wasn't paying attention to his environment. He was very relaxed and didn't have his hand on his firearm while entering or exiting the hotel.

Anyway, my day wasn't worrying about the future of the hotel or whether I would have a job in 90 days. My focus now was making sure that nobody gets hurt or caught during the robbery. I did take note that the camera in the Valet room must be sprayed or moved so when Zeek comes in, nobody would see him. The TASING and taking of the moneybag must go down in seconds in order not to arouse any attention. It would be out of sight of traffic and the driver of the truck.

Later in the day I went outside to see if Joe was comfortable with what he had observed. I mentioned to him that the final thing I must do is move the camera in the valet room on that day. He agreed and was satisfied.

The day had been full of speculations and sadness. The atmosphere in the hotel was very distant and everyone was staying in their own space. I guess this was normal after finding out that your future was in limbo. This would have been a perfect day to pull the robbery off because nobody was giving much attention to anything.

Anyway, it was back to the business of serving the guests. I had a call to take two guests to their room and both were men of the Cloth (Bishops). During our conversation on the way up they did not appear to be gay. This thought left my mind when I opened the door and there was one bed. It wasn't odd when you see two women share a bed, but two men create a negative impression.

"Hey buddy, which side of the bed you want?" said one guy. The other one responded, "It doesn't matter as long as we're together, I'm fine."

This was only one typical adventurous experience being a Bellman. There are always things you see that must go unnoticed.

Well, like I said, the operation of the hotel went on as usual and everyone was trying to keep their spirits up. We were constantly reminded by Management that our service was dependent on if the Church Convention would come back to our hotel as host. Housekeepers were being left nice tips when they went to clean rooms. Even our Room Servers and Dining Room employees were benefiting handsomely from the guests. It was a win-win situation for everyone, especially the Bell staff.

The week had ended and it was just a couple of days before Joe, Zeek and I would pull off one of the most daring robberies the hotel had experienced. I had never heard of such a robbery occurring in any hotel of this magnitude. The adrenaline rush through my body gave me a great sensation when I thought of how much money we would receive if successful.

It was countdown and we had to hold one last meeting to finalize everything such as; deflecting the camera, who's picking up Zeek after the snatch, and where we're going to stash the cash afterwards...

The night before the Brinks pick-up, we held our last meeting at my house. I chilled two bottles of Moët and prepared my favorite dish of shrimp linguine and Alfredo sauce. I wanted it to be a relaxed atmosphere. After all, a full belly makes the mind clear. Although Joe and Zeek seemed nervous when they arrived, the aroma of my food gave them comfort and anticipation. I even had a Blunt (joint) for Zeek to enjoy while we held our pow-wow.

The main thing we had to discuss was who and where Zeek was going to get picked up. My suggestion was someone who would be neutral to either of our welfare. After giving thought to a number of ladies, we all agreed that a girl named Re-Re would be a perfect fit. Re-Re was a lesbian who had hustling qualifications. Her motto was 'Get Your Money By Any Means Necessary', a mentality we needed. She had been to prison several times and was not scared to go back. We all knew she was an opportunist who was willing to do anything or the sake of a dollar. We ended the meeting and left to find her.

Our desire was to see if she would be willing to partake in this role as our getaway driver. We had already decided that I would take a broom and move the camera in the valet room where the TASING would go down. Bringing someone else into the mix at this stage was positive, we thought, because they wouldn't know all of the details. The less you know of a situation, the less you can tell someone.

We arrived at Re-Re's house when she was just getting ready to leave. After explaining our motives to her she immediately said, "Okay, fellows let me get this right…you want me to park two blocks from the hotel and wait for Zeek to transport him to a safe-house with a bag of cash. I'll be glad to do this only…if we're dividing everything equally. I think it's fair since we'll all get the same time if caught."

I didn't have any opposition to splitting the money four ways. After all, it would be velvet if we were successful. Her role would be critical to Zeek getting away without notice. So we all agreed and the case was closed.

After discussing where and when the pick-up would occur, we had to narrow down a time. The Brinks truck arrived at the same time every week, so we assumed they were on schedule. We all concluded that we would base the time on what we had witnessed over the months. We gave each other a hug of solidarity and parted company.

Today was the day...I woke up realizing that all my financial burdens would be gone. Yes, the day had finally come when we would pull off one of the most discrete robberies I could imagine. Before I left for work, I sat down and spoke with my mother.

"Mom, this afternoon, be looking out for Zeek knocking at the back door. He's going to be dropping off a bag to you. Please put it up until I get home and don't answer the door for nobody."

She kind of looked at me startled as if she knew I was up to something wrong and said, "I don't want to know what's going on son, but I'm resting assured that you won't put me in any danger. I'll do this for you and hope you're not putting yourself in trouble."

I wanted to be honest with her because she realized that I was a hustler growing up, but I felt relieved when she didn't want to know. After all, if anything went wrong, I didn't want her to be a conspirator. Anyone having knowledge of this robbery would be charged.

When I arrived at work, everything was tranquil in the hotel. Most of the convention guests had checked out the previous day. All the Bellmen were sitting around waiting for the Church of God in Christ Officials to wrap up their finale meeting so we could get their luggage out of storage. I knew that during this transition I had to move the camera in the valet room that was adjacent to the Bell-Closet. I immediately accomplished this task when I served my first guest.

It would be any minute before the Brinks truck would arrive and I began getting the jitters. Anxiety began to set in on me as the minutes passed. I knew I had to stay calm so I wouldn't arouse any suspicion, so I left the lobby and went outside. As I did, I noticed the Brinks truck pulling in along the side of the hotel. I gave a glance across the street and saw Zeek dressed in woman's attire waiting to make his move. He said he was going to use a disguise, but I was amazed that he went to this length to make everything perfect.

I went back to the hotel with confidence that everything was going to go alright. I immediately had a Front when I arrived at the Bell Stand, so I grabbed a luggage cart and headed toward the elevators. My mind was still racing on the day's event. I arrived at the guest's room and loaded their luggage on my cart and we headed back down to the lobby.

As I got off the elevator, I noticed panic in the lobby. Everyone seemed hysterical as LP (Loss Prevention) Officers were running to the back of the hotel. The Front Desk Clerks were standing in amazement as I approached. "What's going on you all? What's the excitement?" I said. Suddenly, I heard a siren approaching the hotel and my heart dropped to my feet. I immediately thought that the Brinks pick-up man was able to use his firearm against Zeek. However, this was not the case. The Manager came inside the lobby to tell us that the Brinks man was stunned and his moneybag was snatched while he was incapacitated.

Well, I was relieved when a witness came into the hotel and described seeing a woman come out of the Valet door going up the street in a hurry.

"She was carrying a large shopping bag. Moments later I saw the Valet attendant knocking on the Brinks truck telling the driver there has been a robbery," she said.

At this time, I rolled my cart outside to load the guest's luggage. FBI and local Police had surrounded the hotel looking for a suspect, but she was long gone. EMS was on the scene attending to the Brinks pick-up man. I knew he was feeling uncomfortable because I had a TASER demonstrated on me. Besides some pain and stiffness for a few days, I knew he would be alright.

Words could not say how much joy I was feeling at this time. Everything seemed to have worked out perfectly. I just couldn't wait to get home to see the prize.......TO BE CONTINUED.

About the Author

Sherman Cain was born and raised in St. Louis, Missouri. He was the youngest of five boys and one girl; who was the oldest. While his mother was a strong disciplinarian, Sherman's older brothers were an influence on the challenges he would experience in life.

One of Sherman's brothers went into the modeling industry and moved to California to pursue a desire to become a Hollywood actor. Although he was able to appear in a few sitcoms, his acting career was short-lived.

His endeavors gave Sherman a long life aspiration to someday follow his brother's footsteps and become successful. This is when Sherman begins writing short stories and poems that were not noticed by anyone. Most of the stories would be of imaginary characters Sherman created in his mind.

Not realizing that some of Hollywood's best movies were produced by gifted writers, Sherman knew he didn't have a support team to encourage him forward.

As he grew older, Sherman put writing aside and concentrated on the American Dream to finish school, get a great job, get married, and start a family. After all those accomplishments, Sherman moved to California where his desire to write this novel became a reality.

Now, his next adventure is to write a pilot for the marvelous story of THE HOTEL BELLMAN.

Made in the USA
Lexington, KY
19 August 2015